THE ANOINTEDS

The Hartfords'
Deception

By: T.H. Land

All scripture quotations displaying KJV are from the King James Version of the Bible. In addition, general references to the Bible are also based on King James Version of the Bible.

Text copyright ©2024 by T.H. Land

All rights reserved. Published in the United States by Jai Publishing LLC.

ISBN 979-8-9878113-3-7

The Library of Congress has cataloged the softcover edition of this work as follows:

Land, T.H.

The Anointeds: The Hartfords' Deception/ by T.H. Land

Printed in the United States of America

For with God nothing shall be impossible

(Luke 1:37)

CHAPTER 1

JUST A DREAM OR SOMETHING MORE?

Now he which stablisheth us with you in Christ, and hath anointed us, is God.
(2nd Corinthians 1:21)

It was a pleasant, cool, breezy evening in Oldsville Terrace. The birds had retired from singing for the evening. The owls were out full force watching over the city with one eye opened and the other closed.

Skylar and Zoey's neighbor Mr. Fico stepped out on his porch to grab his newspaper—which he had forgotten to bring in earlier that day. Mr. Paul was turning off the sign on his Pizzeria that read OPEN. There was a calm stillness in the air. All seemed tranquil in the little town of Oldsville Terrace… or *so it appeared!*

Sisters Zoey and Skylar had already gone to bed for the evening. Zoey had a cat clock hanging on the wall. Its tail wagged in unison with the clock's second hand. It swung back and forth signaling that it was 3:00 AM. The cool breeze outside effortlessly tossed their handmade bird house from side to side. The wind caressed the water in the inflatable pool. It created a slight ripple as the light from the moon glistened over it!

Suddenly, a heavy darkness filled Skylar and Zoey's room! It was accompanied by a thick fog. Skylar looked closer, in an attempt to unveil what was hidden in the haze.

What is going on? she wondered.

As Skylar wandered around in the mist, as the room grew increasingly darker! Slowly, but surely the fog seeped through the vent and the corners of the door. It managed to overshadow the entire room!

The darkness was drawn together as if it was making a sweet melody. As Skylar made her way towards it, she could see that it was forming not one—or two—but *four* figures!

The clumps of darkness all unified and each began to take the form of a person! They all varied in size and shape and appeared to stand in order—one taller than the next! Skylar was intrigued by what she saw!

She surprisingly felt *no fear* and was strangely captivated by the figures.

They presented themselves as peaceful, kind, friendly even! In a moment's notice, however, everything changed! The four figures abruptly reached out to grab her! Her curiosity diminished as suddenly as helium releasing from a balloon, and fear took its place!

She was now running from the very thing that she once was drawn to! She searched her mind, pondering over who she could call out to for help! Her Grandma Victdamol was the most *gifted* member of her family! She had heard of the many experiences her Grandma V had with dealing with the dark things of this world! *Why would this be an exception?* she thought.

Loudly she shrieked, "Grandma V! Grandma V! Help!"

Skylar was met with an eerie silence! The figures were moving in closer and closer; she could feel their hot breath upon her neck! She dared not look back at her assailants, knowing that they couldn't be too far behind.

Besides it would only slow me down! she reasoned. Skylar could now see her surroundings clearly. She was still in her room, and she glanced around hastily and saw Zoey fast asleep! She made a desperate plea in hopes that her sister would hear her shouting and wake up!

"Help Zoey!" Her voice cracked as she attempted to force those two words out of her mouth! It surprised Skylar that speaking required every inch of energy she could muster!

"Zoey!" She bellowed again as she gasped and collapsed helplessly on the ground.

One of the figures made a final attempt to grab her, but at that EXACT moment, Zoey was shaking Skylar in the *natural realm,* and she was suddenly awakened out of the dream!

Skylar opened her eyes and to her relief, her twin sister Zoey was standing on the side of her bed.

Zoey *sensed* in the *spirit* that her sister needed her help! The twins always had this type of connection for as long as they could remember. They were often able to *sense* when one needed the other.

"Are you okay Skylar?" Zoey asked sympathetically. "Are you having that nightmare again?"

Skylar had been having the *exact* same dream—for months! Skylar wondered what the four figures symbolized.

She looked at her sister with tears in her eyes. "Yes Zoey, but the dream feels *more* real. The figures seemed..." Skylar's eyes zeroed in on her sister's. She hesitated for a moment, then gazed around the room as if the figures had somehow escaped from her dream and may overhear her. Her voice was now a whisper, "*closer!*"

Zoey sat on the bed with a baffled look on her face. Skylar was aware that what she said sounded crazy. How could a dream feel *close?* However, she knew that what she was feeling was valid. Her eyes were now stretched as they darted from side to side. "I think something is very wrong! I just don't know what it is!" Skylar admitted.

****

The twins lived in a town called Oldsville Terrace. Oldsville Terrace was known for its fresh oranges, beautiful scenery, and the smell of crisp peach cobbler year-round! In the summer, the days were hot, but the evenings always managed to have a nice, cool breeze!

The town was small and almost everyone knew each other, from Mailman Dave to Mr. Sparks the baker, not to mention Miss Mary, the owner of *Mary's Sweet Dessert Shop!* Days were often filled with children's innocent screams during water gun fights, hopscotch victories, and shouts of triumph on the baseball field!

Evenings were frequently shared sitting around the dinner table—rehashing the events of the day, while later being tucked away with a good bedtime story! You could say Oldsville Terrace was a typical American town off the coast. In the quiet corners of Oldsville Terrace however, lived something special, veiled…mysterious even!

There were Christians *chosen* by *God* known as Anointeds! Anointeds were special people who were called by *God* to combat the dark things of this world! One set of Anointeds was a family called the Hartfords. Skylar and Zoey were members of the Hartford family. The matriarch of the Hartford family was their grandma, otherwise known as Grandma Victdamol or simply Grandma V. Their family came from a unique line of people that had the favor of *God* shine upon them for generations, because of their obedience to *God*.

****

It was now morning, and the family cookout was in just a few hours. The girls were looking forward to having some good food!

Skylar decided to take the focus off the mystery of her dream and put her attention on something that she knew the answer to—what she was wearing to the cookout! She hopped out of bed and started getting ready.

CHAPTER 2

THE FAMILY COOKOUT!

Skylar and Zoey had just arrived at *the celebration.* They had always loved family cookouts. The smell of the hot dogs sizzling on the grill, the glistening of the barbecue sauce falling off the ribs and the grill marks across the burgers always brought back great family memories!

They could hardly wait until the *grill master* (their dad) pulled the hot dogs off the grill. They were always first in line …well, maybe second. Their little sister, Abby, often managed to squeeze her way between her sisters and plant herself right in front of her dad! It baffled the twins' minds at how their sister's timing was always impeccable!

But this time their dad wasn't manning the grill. Their dad was stuck in Europe on a work trip, so their dad's cousin was cooking. Of course, it wasn't the same for them, but they were still happy to see their family!

Skylar and Zoey sat back and observed their family's celebration. This time, the family came together to celebrate with their uncle! He was retiring from the military! Both their aunt and uncle were great to have around, but their daughter Lizzy was another story!

Lizzy was Skylar and Zoey's age, and she had always been jealous of the twins. She resented them because they had siblings, and she was an only child. It was ironic, because Skylar and Zoey often found themselves wondering what it would be like to be Lizzy.

Lizzy was spoiled rotten! She was always getting her way! The girls wondered how it would feel to have all their parents' attention. Their parents seemed to be focused more on their two younger siblings.

Nevertheless, Skylar and Zoey understood that their sister and brother were younger, and they needed their mom and dad's assistance more. Although, they did wish that their parents would distribute their time more evenly among all their children.

The girls' neighbor, Mr. Fico, was invited to the cookout as well. Mr. Fico never got married and he didn't have any children. Nevertheless, he was still good with kids! The girls weren't sure what type of work he did, but it kept him gone quite a bit. They wondered if this was the reason he didn't get married.

Skylar and Zoey watched as Mr. Fico ran tirelessly around while Abby chased him with a water gun. Their mom always accused Mr. Fico of being a big kid! It was moments like that when they understood what their mom meant. The laughter of Abby and the other children echoed throughout the park as Mr. Fico and the other kids managed to dodge Abby's water gun at every turn.

"No fair!" Abby squealed as she grabbed a second water gun in hopes that she would have better luck with two!

Meanwhile, Lizzy was watching Skylar and Zoey intently as if she was a hunter observing its prey! She plastered a big smile on her face and skipped her way across the yard over to them.

"Hey." Lizzy groaned as she wiped some cherry popsicle juice off her chin.

Zoey rolled her eyes and chose to completely ignore Lizzy.

The twins wondered why their cousin was wearing a pink dress. The dress was more appropriate for a pageant than a barbecue! She always believed everyone was beneath her, so it was no surprise that she wanted to dress the part.

"Hi Lizzy!" Skylar forced her voice to sound chipper. Skylar always tried to be friendly with Lizzy, but even she had a hard time dealing with her cousin's constant negative attitude. Over the years Lizzy had managed to get even worse.

Zoey did what she always did, she got as far away from Lizzy as she could! She was able to breeze right past her without as much as a 'hello'.

Skylar glared over at her sister as Zoey did a victory dance and made her way to the baseball field. Lizzy turned to see what Skylar could possibly be looking at that could be more important than her!

She whipped her head back around, "What are you looking at?" she questioned with her arms folded.

Skylar realized that she too was now ignoring her cousin, however not on purpose. "Nothing," she insisted while shrugging her shoulders and turning her focus back to Lizzy.

Lizzy's frown turned back to a smile now that the attention was back on her.

Skylar wondered what she and Lizzy could possibly talk about; after all, they had nothing in common!

Lizzy observed Skylar with satisfaction on her face. "Anyway, are you ready for summer?"

"Yes, I am!" Skylar replied enthusiastically. Finally, a topic they both could agree on—summer!

Lizzy began to twirl her hair around her fingertips. "Well, you know Daddy and Mommy are taking me to Columbia. I've been studying Spanish, so they want me to experience the culture as well. Have you ever been to Colombia?" She had a snobbish tone.

Skylar knew that her cousin was aware that she had barely been out of Oldsville Terrace—much less the country!

"No Lizzy, I've never been." Skylar was unsuccessful at hiding the annoyance in her voice.

"Oh, what about New York?" Lizzy retorted.

"NO."

"California?"

"NO."

Lizzy threw her hands up in the air.

"Have you at least been to Florida?"

"NO!" Skylar stomped her foot on the ground.

Just then, Grandma Victdamol placed her hand on Skylar's shoulder. "Lizzy, I haven't seen my granddaughter in months, would you give us some time together?"

Skylar grabbed her Grandma Victdamol and hugged her tightly. She was embracing her for two reasons: because she missed her, and because she was *thankful* that she saved her from that hideous conversation with her cousin Lizzy.

Lizzy annoyingly shrugged her shoulders and set her eyes on her next target—Abby!

"Grandma V, it's so good to see you!" Skylar was still squeezing her grandma.

"I saw you in distress and figured you needed a little bit of help," her grandma winked.

Lizzy wasn't related to her. Grandma V was Skylar and Zoey's maternal grandma. The girls' dad and Lizzy's dad were brothers.

Skylar and Zoey's mom strolled over with her bright yellow sun hat. She knew that it was hideous, but she wasn't wearing it for fashion. The hat was great for keeping the sun from bearing down on her delicate skin.

"Hello Mother." Their mom placed a bland kiss on Grandma Victdamol's cheek.

"Hello sweetheart, I absolutely love your hat!" Grandma V took the liberty of touching the rim of it.

Skylar shook her head from side to side. *Only someone that is almost a century old could appreciate a hat like that.* Skylar thought.

She unknowingly chuckled out loud at her thoughts. Both Mom and Grandma Victdamol gave a scolding look at Skylar, and she quickly exited the conversation and decided to play baseball with the other kids.

"Hailey, it would be great if you brought the girls out to church sometimes. Everybody's been asking about all of you," Grandma V hesitantly informed.

Mom rolled her eyes and began to ponder on how to respond to her mother. She felt as if Grandma V was always trying to *force God* on her. She knew this was Grandma Victdamol's way of saying, "you need to get your life together!"

"You know, Mother, I've been so busy." She said while refusing to make eye contact with Grandma V. "It's tough having four kids, working a fulltime job, and being a wife. After all, you live so far, it's a day's journey just to get to church," she retorted.

Now their grandma did live out in the country. However, their mom exaggerated on it being *a day's journey.*

Grandma Victdamol shook her head from side to side in a manner that was reprimanding their mother, even though she didn't say a word. She always thought that maybe she pampered Hailey too much when she was a child. After all, she was an only child and Grandma Victdamol was a few years shy of being fifty when she found out that *God* was blessing her with a bundle of joy!

She would often laugh and call herself Sarah, because she conceived at an older age! Like Sarah (Abraham's wife) *God* too promised Grandma Victdamol that she would be blessed with a child. However, unlike Sarah, her husband Stanley was *no* Abraham! Grandma V dismissed the bad memories and gazed at her daughter.

"Just as *God* makes time for you— you must make time for *Him!*"

Hailey knew where this was headed. Mother was going to lecture her pertaining to her relationship with *God*—or lack thereof! She scanned the gathering to see if there was anything that could pull her away from the conversation.

"Look at me!" Grandma Victdamol firmly gripped her daughter's chin. "*God* is a loving *God*, but *He* is also a *jealous* one. Make time for *Him*, you never know when you may need *Him* to make time for you!"

For a moment, there was something about her mother's tone that rang true to her, almost like an ominous warning! But Hailey's stubbornness got the best of her! She refused to be chastised like a child. She gently pushed her mother's hand from her chin. Hailey quickly devised a plan to make her escape! She surveyed the park in search of an escape from the conversation.

Perfect! she thought while looking over at a group of kids. "Listen, I'd love to discuss this, but I've got to see what those kids are up to!" She brushed passed her mother and began to shout at the kids for tossing water balloons over the table with the desserts.

Grandma V stood there heart broken, but she didn't feel that way for long. *The*

Holy Spirit, The Comforter, surrounded her with love and encouragement. "I'll continue to pray," she declared with gentleness in her voice. She knew that she was in a battle. One of the toughest battles of her life, the battle for her daughter's *soul.* But she also knew that *God* would answer her prayers, and *He* would get Hailey's attention—*one way or another!*

Grandma Victdamol and the girls' mother had a strained relationship for quite some time. Their mom didn't always make the choices that Grandma V hoped she would.

To Grandma Victdamol, choosing *God* was *The Only Choice!* Their mom on the other hand, didn't focus on a relationship with *God anymore.* She viewed Christianity as something *boring. Oh, how wrong she was!*

Their Grandma Victdamol wanted her daughter to carry out *God's* plan for her life, but as she grew older, she began to unfortunately move further and further away from *Him!* She looked at her *calling* or *God's* purpose for her life as an inconvenience of some sorts!

She began to reason things in her mind, and search for explanations on her own. Hailey no longer listened to the voice of the *Holy Spirit.* She allowed negative experiences to overshadow the truth of *God's Word.*

She couldn't see that *God* was always there, and *He* wasn't going anywhere!

Howbeit when he, the Spirit of truth, is come, he will guide you into all truth: for he shall not speak of himself; but whatsoever he shall hear, that shall he speak: and he will show you things to come.

(John 16:13 KJV)

She instead chose to ignore the *Spirit of Truth* and trusted herself and other people. Grandma Victdamol could never pinpoint the exact moment Hailey changed. As a little girl, she loved Sunday School and singing in the choir.

She was eager to learn all she could about *God.* Once she got married and had her third child she began to slowly drift away from the *Word.* She no longer had time for the things of *God.* As time progressed, her distance grew greater. She stopped teaching her children, and became distracted with her day-to-day life, until eventually she moved completely away from being a Christian.

Skylar and Zoey on the other hand, loved *God* and always had faith in *His* existence. They were eager to learn about *Him*. *God* had a calling on the girls' lives, and they (unlike their mother) were eager to walk in it! At a young age, they began to spend time in *God's Word*.

And ye shall seek me, and find me, when ye shall search for me with all your heart.
(Jeremiah 29:13)

CHAPTER 3

NARRATOR'S CORNER

Did you know that reading God's word helped Skylar and Zoey grow closer to the things of God? Well, it most certainly did and if you seek him, you will grow as well!

Skylar and Zoey were a part of the newest generation of Anointeds, who found favor with *God!* They understood that *God* raised a remnant of people to assist with fighting against the evil in this world, and the Hartfords were a part of that remnant!

I have an interesting fact for you! There are Spiritual Gifts, called *The Nine Gifts of the Spirit. The Gifts of the Spirit* are: *Word of Wisdom, Word of Knowledge, Faith, Gifts of Healing, Working of Miracles, Prophecy, Discerning of Spirits, Divers Kinds of Tongues, and the Interpretation of Tongues.* (You can find out more about these gifts in 1Corinthians 12:1-11.)

The Word of Wisdom is when something pertaining to the future is revealed through the *Spirit of God* to a person. For example, many of the prophets in the *Bible* were warned of impending judgement on a nation.

The Word of Knowledge is information about the present or past that is revealed to an individual by the *Spirit of God.* For example, *Jesus* saw the disciple Nathanael sitting under a fig tree even though he wasn't anywhere near Nathanael. (John1:47-50). Also, there was a Samaritan woman at a well, *Jesus* told her about things she had done in the past, like how many husbands she had and other specific things about her life. (John 4:1-30). This is an example of the *Word of Knowledge!*

The Working of Miracles is when a literal miracle takes place. *Jesus* needed to feed 5,000 people, but there were only five loaves of bread and two fish. The food was multiplied, and all of the people were fed and there was still food left over! This was clearly a miracle. (Mathew 14:13-21). Samson's supernatural strength was also *The Working of Miracles!* Samson wouldn't have been able to kill a thousand Phillistines if it were not for *God* working a miracle. (Judges 15:11-17).

Gift of Faith is supernatural faith! This is when a person trusts in *God* to take complete control of a situation. When Daniel was in the lion's den, he was operating in this gift, and *God* sent an angel to shut the lions' mouths! (Daniel 6)

Now *Discerning of Spirits* is another one of the *Nine Gifts of the Spirit.* This gift is very important as well. *Discerning of Spirits* allows you to know what spirit you're dealing with. It reveals if it's a spirit from *God,* or an evil spirit. This gift can also discern the spirit of a person!

Let's take a look back at the story of Nathanael (also known as Bartholomew), *Jesus* knew the character of Nathanael. He knew he was a good man. *Jesus* could tell which people were children of *God* and who was a child of the devil.

I know what you're wondering, what about *The Gifts of Healing?* Well, this gift is when people are healed from some type of sickness through the power of *God.* There are numerous accounts of where *Jesus* healed people in the *New Testament.* For example, the blind could see, among other healings.

Prophecy is another *Gift of the Spirit.* When this gift moves it can encourage a person and comfort them. Isaiah said he was given words from the Lord to strengthen someone who was going through something. (Isaiah 50:4) When people have a prophetic word, they are often told of things pertaining to the future as well. The last two *Gifts are Divers Kinds of Tongues and Interpretation of Tongues*. *The Gifts of* Tongues is when through the *Holy Spirit*—the person is able to speak in a language they have never learned, for example the Heavenly language. *Interpretation of Tongues* is when the words being spoken are understood.

Did you know that the *Bible* says you can pray and ask for any of the gifts? Yes, this means you! Now, each member of the Hartfords family has operated in at least one of the *Nine Gifts of the Spirit* from time to time.

CHAPTER 4

WILL SHE FALL FOR IT?

The week had breezed by, and it was now the last day of school! Skylar and Zoey cracked open their parents' door and tiptoed across the floor. The girls stopped to gaze at a painting they always admired that their mom had of a rainbow. Looking at that painting always seemed to put a smile on their faces. Their mom's cat, Peepop, was curled up in the corner on the rocking chair.

Peepop opened one eye and watched the girls as they made their way across the cold hardwood floors. They wondered why the floor was so cold even though it was almost summer. Peepop stretched forward her paw and began to sharpen her claws on the flower pillow he was laying on.

"Shh, Peepop!" Zoey whispered, but Peepop continued as if she didn't hear a word.

The twins leaned towards their mom and yelled, "Mom wake up!"

Mom moaned while nudging the girls off her bed with her feet. "Go away!"

"Mom come on! We're going to be late!" Skylar insisted.

Their mom crawled out of bed with a tank top and shorts on. She reached under her bed for her house shoes. *Where are you?* she wondered.

A wet, warm tongue ran across her fingertips. "Yuck! Stop it Shye!" The dog ran out of the room with her fuzzy pink slippers. Skylar and Zoey ran after him calling for him to bring the house shoes back.

Mom stepped slowly onto the cold floor and rose on her tippy toes to prevent her entire feet from being subjected to the cold. All she could think about was her coffee and how much she wanted some.

Zoey had just woken up their little brother Nick and was feeding him. "And how is my favorite baby brother?" She was making funny faces at him and attempted to do her *baby* voice.

Nick poked his bottom lip out and started crying.

"Watch out! Let me." Skylar unstrapped Nick out of his highchair and rocked him back and forth.

"I don't understand why he likes you better. After all, I'm prettier." Zoey admired her reflection in the toaster.

"Can I get my breakfast please?" Abby whined as she stood folding her arms.

"Abby are you ready for first grade next year?" Skylar was still rocking Nick back and forth in her arms.

"I guess so." Abby hadn't put much thought into the coming school year. She had her hands full making sure that Harley Adams didn't steal her favorite box of crayons!

"Do we get to sit in the big kids' seats in first grade?" she inquired with a gleam of hope in her eyes.

In Abby's class, all of the kids sat at round tables that were spread out amongst the classroom. Abby caught glimpses of her sisters' classrooms and saw that they sat at individual desks, and she called it the *big kid's seats!*

"Only if you're good, squirt!" Zoey rustled Abby's hair.

Mom turned the corner with her briefcase in one hand and her reading glasses in the other. "What would I do without you girls? You fixed Abby's hair, fed Nick, and even made a little something for me," she praised while stirring a spoon in her soggy cereal.

Their mom was exhausted from working on the corporate accounts at her job. She was an investment banker for Bartley Bank, which was one of the biggest banks in the world. She had barely enough time to fix her own hair much less anyone else's. She had been working on these accounts for three months straight and it was wearing her out!

Mom looked around and noticed Zoey had cleaned the entire kitchen, vacuumed the living room, and now she was standing in the pantry—organizing it! She was completing all of the household chores, before she even headed to school!

She was occasionally smiling at her mom as she hummed a tune while placing the last can on the shelf. Now Zoey wasn't exactly a morning person, and she certainly didn't volunteer to clean anything! It took Mom repeating herself a minimum of five times before Zoey would clean her side of the room. And let's not talk about her washing her clothes!

One of Mom's eyebrows raised as she ventured into the laundry room, and just as she suspected—Zoey's clothes were washed, folded, and placed on top of the dryer! Their mom knew right away that Zoey was up to something.

Mom thought for a moment and pondered on the possibilities. She quickly eliminated one possibility after another and came to a sobering conclusion.

"You think that I don't know what this is all about?" Mom wagged her finger back and forth. "You want to go to my mother's house after school, but it isn't going to happen!" she grabbed her purse off the counter.

"Mom!" Zoey whined with her bottom lip poked out.

"No way. Your dad will be back in town today." Mom shot Zoey a sympathetic look in her direction. "Besides I have to work late, and I won't have time to take you!"

"But Mom, we can catch the city bus!" Skylar suggested with a smile.

Mom faced Skylar. "Oh, you're in on this as well, I see."

Skylar sunk back in her seat.

"Mother lives too far for you girls to travel on your own!" Mom stared at them with beady little eyes and a wrinkled forehead. She stood, tapping her black heels against their hardwood floor.

"Mom we're eleven, we're not babies anymore. We'll be fine on the bus! Besides, we'll see Dad later tonight!" Zoey responded.

"Oh really?" Mom's attention turned back to Zoey. "The answer is NO!" Mom walked out the door.

Zoey rolled her eyes and slammed her bowl in the sink, causing the milk to splash everywhere!

Skylar shook her head at her sister with disappointment in her eyes. In return, Zoey glared back at Skylar.

Mom peeked her head back inside. "Zoey, that's one of the reasons why you're not going to my mother's house! You say you're not a little kid, but you're acting just like one!" Mom stepped back in and placed her hands on her hips. "You have an attitude problem! Now clean that milk up!"

Their mom was aware of what Zoey had done, even with her back turned!

"Mom, how did you know what Zoey did?" Skylar had a confused look on her face.

Mom winked at Skylar. "Don't you know that all moms have eyes in the back of their heads?" she joked.

Abby had been watching everything that transpired. She walked up to her mom. "Mom, I don't want to wear this outfit!" Abby stomped her feet.

She was behaving in the same manner she saw her big sister behaving—spoiled!

"Furthermore, what did I tell you about setting a good example for Abby? She is your little sister. She's always watching you!" Mom informed.

Skylar went to clean up the mess that Zoey made.

"Thank you, Skylar." Mom nodded.

Zoey was about to stomp out of the room, but a *Word of Wisdom* came to Skylar. She was suddenly aware of what Zoey was about to do, before it happened.

"Don't you dare do that, Zoey, that's so rude!" she scolded her while ringing the cloth tightly in her hands.

Before Zoey could respond, she stopped and pondered on what Skylar had said. She would usually get upset when Skylar would operate in this particular *Gift of the*

Spirit. However, despite her frustration, it often kept her out of trouble.

"Zoey get in the car!" Mom demanded. Their mom did not know what Zoey intended on doing, but by Skylar's reaction she knew it couldn't be good. Zoey grabbed her books and headed to the car.

Their mom leaned forward and whispered in Skylar's ear. "Please be more subtle when operating in the gifts. If you're enemies found out about you, it might put you both in danger."

"If they found out about us, Mom." Skylar turned to face her mom. "You are an Anointed too!"

"No, you must be mentored to become an Anointed. I've never been trained," Mom headed out the door.

"Well, you're still an *Anointed* Mom, and there's nothing you can do about that." Skylar gave a gentle smile. "That's who you are. It's a blessing from *God.*"

"Just get in the car. You're going to be late to school," Mom replied.

CHAPTER 5

IT'S THE LAST DAY OF SCHOOL!

They pulled up to their school. It was over 60 years old, and the appearance confirmed its age. Skylar and Zoey hated the way their school looked! The brick building had begun to crack down the sides and the doors were in badly need of a replacement. There were visible leaks when you walked in the building and each corner wall had 'signature' rust stains engraved on the pipes.

The playground wasn't much better! The basketball court was missing a basketball net on one of the hoops and the baseball field's dugout was flooded from a heavy rain in the early winter, and no one had bothered to drain it. The only things that were up to date were the slides and the swings. You could only imagine the long wait for your turn during recess. Most students resorted to playing tag or dodgeball. Despite all these negatives, their mom and dad made them remain at Grains Elementary School because of the five-star education it provided.

Much of the residence of Oldsville Terrace viewed it as a historical sight, but the girls didn't care. They wanted a more modern look for the school they attended. Although the teachers were good, and they had many friends, their mood always darkened due to their environment. Skylar and Zoey were headed to a new school next year for middle school, so it would no longer be *their* problem. However, they still hoped that the school would experience some positive modifications for Abby and Nick's sake.

They waved goodbye to their mom and started walking Abby to her class. Abby swung around an old, rusted pole with one hand, which made Skylar squirm.

"I don't know why you like playing with that, now you have rust all over your hand," Skylar moaned.

Abby didn't seem to care about the rust; she just loved the breeze against her face as she swung around and around!

A boy by the name of Jake was walking towards the girls. Jake was dubbed the 5th grade bully, and for good reason! He would take kids' desserts out of their lunch boxes and if someone didn't bring dessert, no problem! He made no qualms about taking their lunch money! Jake was taller than most 5th graders—after all, he was *repeating* the grade for the *second* time!

He was a red head with brown eyes and freckles all over his face, and he was rather tall for his age. If you looked really closely, you could even see tiny strands of hair above his lip. The girls didn't understand why Jake liked being so mean. He was the most disliked kid in the 5th grade! The only kids that played with him were the ones that he forced to! Jake was sent to the office so much that Principal Whittaker gave him his own assigned seat in his office.

The girls were so engulfed in their own conversation that they didn't notice Jake slowly approaching. He was like a shark spotting fish from afar.

Zoey looked in Skylar's direction. She was quickly reminded of what happened at home. "I don't appreciate you telling me what to do!" Zoey brushed past Skylar.

"Zoey, if you stomped out of the room after making that mess, Mom may not have let you go to Grandma Vs at all this summer!"

"Well, if it isn't ugly and the ugliest twin. Is it Halloween already?" Jake forced his way between the girls as he laughed hysterically. If no one else found his jokes humorous, it didn't bother him much! He was sure to be his own audience!

"You better shut up!" Abby yelled with her fists up in the air.

"Wow! There are three of you?" Jake stood and snarled. "You better *shut up*," he repeated in a mocking tone as he leaned in towards Abby.

"That does it!" Zoey began to punch one fist in her other hand.

Skylar stood in front of her. "Remember who you are Zoey! Remember—be on the side of *good!*"

Skylar turned Zoey away from Jake.

Zoey took a deep breath, twirled her ponytail around the tip of her finger, and calmly walked away as she mumbled under her breath.

"You better be lucky my sister didn't use her gift!" Abby leaned towards Jake with both of her hands stretched back.

Jake shook his head from side to side and raised his eyebrows. "What did you say little girl?" He wondered what Abby meant by the comment.

Skylar pulled Abby behind her. "She's just babbling, that's all."

Jake glanced at her with a puzzled look on his face. "Whatever!" Jake spotted Tommy Taylor, the smallest kid in their class. "Hey Tommy, what am I having for lunch today?" He reached for Tommy's lunch. Skylar was grateful that Jake's focus was off of them. However, she felt terrible for Tommy!

Skylar waited for Jake to be out of view before she bent down on one knee and pulled Abby towards her. "And how do you know about *Spiritual Gifts?*" she interrogated.

Zoey walked back over to her sisters. "Skylar, she isn't stupid. She watches us. She sees the supernatural happening all around her!"

"Abby, anything that *God* allows you to do, is not to be done out of anger. Besides, gifts only move as *God* allows." Skylar could see the confused look on Abby's face. But she continued, "and it doesn't work the way you think." Abby looked even more confused, but Skylar wasn't sure how to explain it.

"I only have one question…" Abby started impatiently tapping her right foot.

Skylar and Zoey quickly huddled around Abby.

"Why don't I have any gifts?" Abby dug her foot in the sand with both hands behind her back.

Skylar and Zoey peered at one another; they were baffled by the question. Abby had a good point. After all, she was a Hartford! By the time they reached her age, they were already having experiences and learning how to operate in some of the *Gifts of the Spirit*. They both shrugged their shoulders.

"We don't know. That's a question for Grandma V." Zoey ran her hand through her hair.

Skylar's phone rang and it was Grandma V calling. Skylar held one finger up to indicate to her sisters to stop speaking. The kids at school were so loud that she could barely hear through the phone. Skylar quickly responded and hung up the phone.

"Who was it?" Zoey asked.

"It was Grandma V. She said to come to her house right now! I could barely hear her, but she needs to tell us something in person."

"What's wrong?" Abby asked.

"I'm not sure but, we've got to go!" Skylar said. Skylar and Zoey grabbed Abby's hand and ran off the school grounds towards the nearest city bus stop!

****

Mom had just dropped Nick off to daycare. Nick loved his daycare teacher! He was excited that he would still be attending daycare during the summer.

"Skylar doesn't know what she's talking about. I'm not ashamed of being an Anointed, I'm just different! I don't operate in any *Gift of the Spirit*!" Their Mom began to reminisce about when she was her girls' age.

She pictured a happier time; a time when she came from Sunday School and her dad was waiting on the porch with her first pet! He had it hidden behind his back and told Hailey to close her eyes. When she opened them, there was a beautiful gray bunny moving its nose from side to side. She burst with joy as she hugged her dad!

She smiled as she reminisced. She hadn't seen her dad since she was a kid. One day he was *there* and the next, he was *gone*, no explanation! Come to think of it, her rabbit, who was considered her closest friend at the time, left shortly after her dad did.

How strange! she thought.

At the time, she was going through something, and she really needed her dad and her best friend, but neither one of them was anywhere to be found!

Her mother was left to pick up the pieces for both Hailey's dad and her rabbit's absence. As time went by, she found herself able to recall fewer and fewer *good* memories of her dad. She wasn't sure if it was because she was getting older or if there were so few memories of him that were worth remembering. She felt the tears slowly streaming down her face and quickly wiped them away. She had unfortunately gotten used to suppressing her feelings.

"Okay Hailey, hold it together." She scolded herself and dismissed her feelings, just as she had done as a child. She turned the radio up and began listening to music.

CHAPTER 6

TRAINING BEGINS!

"*Wow Grandma, I've never seen you be mean to anyone,*" Skylar stated disappointingly.

"Oh, my Skylar, there is much to learn in so little time. My dear friend outside has not yet decided if he will be on the side of good or evil. He is what we call an *Undutched*. He is lukewarm. He is neither hot nor cold, and as long as he is an *Undutched,* he *cannot* and *will not* be trusted!" Grandma Victdamol scooted over to a very old wooden rocking chair and sat down.

"Grandma how did you know that he was Undutched?" Zoey asked as she pushed her bangs out of her face.

"Well," Grandma V adjusted her posture in her rocking chair. "*God* allowed me to operate in the *Gift of Discerning of*

Spirits. It let me know who Rainn really is. It's a powerful gift! Only *God* knows the heart of a man. It's the gift that can give us a glimpse into who we are dealing with. It discerns the human spirit of a person, when angels are present, or demons."

The girls stood with their mouths open in amazement.

"Wow that's cool. I wonder if that gift could tell me what Sally James really thinks of me." Abby's mouth twisted to the left. "She says we're friends but I'm not so sure. She's always pushing me down and being mean!" Abby placed her pointer finger on her chin.

"You don't need a gift to figure that out squirt," Zoey answered while placing Abby on her lap, whom, by the way, *still* appeared bewildered.

Grandma V lived in a wooden house. There were pictures lined up along one side of the wall. The frames housed smiling faces of family members, which spanned over 150 years! The interior of the home was older as well.

There was plastic over the sofa and beads hanging in the doorway which led to the kitchen. Zoey and Skylar hated the way the beads sounded and how they brushed against their faces. As a result, they would only enter the kitchen if one of the twins held the beads bawled up in her hand as the other eased in. They would then switch to allow the other to enter the kitchen!

Skylar and Zoey followed Grandma V into the kitchen. She glanced over her shoulder as the girls followed their routine of holding the beads and doing the *beads dance* as Grandma V called it. Grandma V giggled to herself thinking how ridiculous the girls were for doing that every time. Grandma V grabbed a plate of macadamia and chocolate chip cookies.

Grandma V always had to bake both cookies because Skylar's favorite was macadamia, and Zoey only ate chocolate chip. Abby, on the other hand, ate any cookie she could get her hands on. The girls grabbed their cookies off the plate and quickly followed Grandma V out of the kitchen and back into the family room.

Skylar and Zoey looked around the room, and both sets of eyes landed on Grandma V's parrot, Penelope. She was sitting in her cage, swinging back and forth repeating, "Goodbye, goodbye" over and over.

The girls tried their best to ignore Grandma V's parrot. They were never too fond of Penelope and the fact that she was so rude, did little to help alter their feelings.

They knew that Penelope kept repeating 'goodbye' over and over, because she didn't like it when they came over to Grandma V's house. Penelope was jealous! Grandma walked over to Penelope and handed her a cracker as a peace offering.

"Grandma, why did you need us to come? What's wrong?" Zoey stuffed the cookies in her mouth.

"That's just it; I don't know yet. A *Word of Wisdom* came to me that evil was headed to Oldsville Terrace and that we needed to prepare for these enemies! The time has come for me to mentor the two of you. I didn't want to go into this with you girls being so young, but I have no choice! We must heed the warning and prepare!"

Grandma V stood to her feet and stepped through her back door, and the girls followed. This was the first time the girls had noticed that her house was positioned on a huge rock. It reminded them of the rock that Rainn had given them, and this scripture came to their remembrance.

Therefore, whosoever heareth these sayings of mine, and doeth them, I will liken him unto a wise man, which built his house upon a rock: And the rain descended, and the floods came, and the winds blew, and beat upon that house; and it fell not: for it was founded upon a rock.
(Mathew 7:24-25)

Skylar and Zoey perceived that one of the reasons Rainn gave them the rocks was that it symbolized being a wise person and following *Jesus!* It was a reminder to walk in *obedience* and if trouble came, it would not overtake them. The girls were certainly seeing more *good* in Rainn than *bad!*

There was a waterfall near Grandma's backyard. The sound of the water flowing over the rocks managed to enhance an already serene environment. Zoey and Skylar immediately smiled when they heard the sound of the water flowing.

"Lay back in the lawn chairs girls and relax," Grandma V pulled her rocking chair beside their lawn chairs. She then closed her eyes and began to drift into a deep sleep. The girls, one by one, did the same.

The girls slowly *awoke* in a *dream realm*, but something was different about this dream—they were all sharing the SAME dream! All of the girls looked at one another amazed and bewildered. Grandma V gave a warm smile. "*God* trains me and teaches me things—sometimes in dreams!" Grandma V's voice echoed in the dream realm. The girls observed the radiant colors, everything seemed much more vibrant than it did in the *natural realm*!

They began to walk through a fog. It was similar to thick, fluffy clouds. For a moment, the girls took the opportunity to dance around in this cottony playground, sort of speak. But they quickly lost sight of one another. The fog grew so thick that they could no longer see their hands in front of their faces. What was lots of fun initially, instantly became a state of panic!

"Where did everyone go?" Abby whined.

"Enough!" Grandma V yelled and the fog quickly ceased. She had been trained in this realm through dreams and visions since her youth. She knew that it was necessary for them to experience the darkness while training. This would teach them how to battle in the *natural world.*

The ground was like clay and the sky appeared as an array of vibrant watercolors. If the girls didn't know better, they would have thought the sky was one large oil painting! Aside from the obvious disparities, this realm still managed to have a level of normalcy.

They still heard the sound of birds chirping, saw the sun shining bright, and they could hear Grandma V's waterfall off in the distance. The birds, however, sounded as if they were singing a song that wasn't earthly. They were singing in a pitch that the girls had never heard before! The wind blew cool air and wrapped around them as if it were a large blanket.

"Grandma V, it's almost like everything's alive—even the wind!" Skylar stretched forth her hand in the air. The breeze blew through her fingers as if it were moving in agreement with her.

Grandma V glimpsed up at the sky. "Oh, but it is my dear Skylar. It is!"
As they stepped on a thin colorful bridge, there was a rainbow right above their heads.
Zoey pointed in the direction of the rainbow. "Do you think there's a pot of gold over there?" They all giggled and continued to venture forward.
"Girls, once we come out on the other side, it will be a world unlike this one! There, you will see some of the dark side of the *spiritual realm.*"
Grandma V took their hands and closed her eyes. The bridge began to float away from the light! The world that they had just experienced was now off in the distance. The bridge was slowly moving towards darkness. It finally rested on a large land mass made of tar. One by one they stepped off the bridge.
"Grandma V my feet are sticking to the ground!" Abby whined as she attempted unsuccessfully to walk forward. Quickly the ground turned to black gravel and her feet

were no longer stuck. Abby went flying backwards onto the ground!

Skylar rushed to her aid. "Are you okay?"

"Yes, I'm just happy I'm not stuck anymore!" she giggled.

With a glance to ensure that Abby was okay, Grandma V continued. "You must not only learn to fight on our terms, but you must also learn to fight in the enemies' camp as well! You cannot allow your environment to distract or discourage you! Let your *light,* shine regardless of where you are!"

Skylar and Zoey looked at one another. They had just heard Rainn mention the *Light.* But they didn't dare mention anything about Rainn to Grandma V.

Grandma V hurried forward. "Come children, you mustn't tarry. We must get through the woods and out of the forest before the Javas awake!"

"Javas? That can't be good!" Zoey swallowed hard; her eyes darted from side to side.

They continued to travel through the woods at a swift pace. There was every creature imaginable there. The girls ducked their heads, toddled from left to right, and even hurdled over a few toads. They were grateful that they could only hear the sounds of some of the other creatures and couldn't see them! They weren't sure they could go any further if they could have seen what had made those frightening noises!

They finally made their way to the other side of the woods and entered the forest.

The journey didn't take as long as it would have if they were in the *natural realm*. Several miles were covered in the span of about twenty minutes! The girls remained quiet as they journeyed through the forest, one question kept pondering over and over in their minds.

Finally, Skylar mustered the courage to ask. "Grandma, what are Javas?" she inquired, although she wasn't sure if she really wanted to know.

"You'll know soon enough," Grandma V said.

The girls didn't like the sound of that! And with a wave of the hand to discourage any further conversation, Grandma V resumed with the lesson.

"Skylar, *pray* that this tree be turned into something else."

Grandma V was referring to the large tree in the middle of the road blocking the path. Skylar examined the tree. It was large with thick roots. The tree was big enough that it sat awkwardly in the middle of the road.

"Grandma V, you know that we can't change the form of anything." Skylar turned to Grandma V with a wrinkle on her forehead.

"No Skylar, we can't, but *God* can do anything! There was a time in the *Bible* when *God* spoke to Moses and his brother Aaron. *God* told Aaron to cast down a rod before Pharoah. *God* did a miracle—*He* turned the rod into a serpent! *Jesus* did many miracles as well, like the time *He* turned the water into wine!" Grandma V smiled. "These were all *miracles* that had taken place!"

The girls' eyes lit up! They were taken back by what amazing miracles *God and Jesus* had done in the *Bible*!

Grandma V closed her eyes and silently prayed. When she finished praying, the tree transformed into an elephant!

"Wow!" Abby leaped in the air. "Can I pet it?"

Grandma V shook her head, and the elephant returned to its original state—a tree.

"Let me tell you a little bit about the *spiritual realm*." Grandma V explained while brushing the dirt off a log and sitting.

"Spiritual beings can appear invisible and make noises at times. But Javas are visible, and they look human. Javas are typically short in height, about four feet tall and they have a signature dent in their noses. One challenge is that they can appear extremely friendly! This often puts people at ease.

"It is written that even the devil can come as an angel of light." Grandma V gathered the girls around her. "This is why the *Gifts of Discernment* is crucial! It will allow you to look beyond what you *see, think, or feel!* You will be able to identify what spirit you're dealing with—good or evil."

Grandma V stared into the girls' eyes. "With humans, you can discern if the human spirit is good or bad, like I said earlier about Rainn! When we do not operate in discernment or choose to ignore it, unfortunately it's possible to be deceived! Javas do a great job of appearing good! That's often all they need to do to deceive an Anointed or a Miran.

"Be aware of Javas at all times! There are also Hazils who are actually human, but they are evil. They often will try to deceive Anointeds, but you must always trust the *Holy Spirit,*" Grandma V stressed as she stood gazing off in the distance. It was as if a distant memory made its way back.

The girls waited patiently for Grandma V to continue. The silence only lasted for a moment, yet the awkwardness of it all felt like an eternity. It was as if Grandma V read their minds, and she immediately placed her attention back on the task at hand. "However, Anointeds *do* have very strong instincts and are not easily deceived."

Abby rubbed her nose as if she was wiping the snot away after a good cry. "They all sound scary Grandma V!"

"I understand how it can sound frightening, but you girls are Anointeds! Remember, with *God* you have nothing to fear!" Grandma V gave a comforting smile to the girls. "Skylar, it's your turn!"

Skylar stood firm and prayed with *faith!* The tree slowly spun in a circle and transformed into a giant duck.

"WOW!" Abby squealed.

"Good job!" Zoey applauded.

Grandma V winked at Skylar. "Well done. You have a lot more faith than I anticipated!" The duck changed back to a tree.

Zoey brushed past her twin. "Now it's my turn!" She began to pray.

A flock of birds suddenly appeared above Zoey's head. They started to squawk loudly. Zoey quickly became distracted. Her focus was on the presence of the birds and whether or not they would poop on her head!

She began to fan her hands back and forth. The wind started spinning around the tree and suddenly the dust cleared. The tree turned into a giant, black bat! The bat was flying straight for Zoey!

"Zoey don't get distracted! Just as *God* transformed the rod to a snake for Moses and Aaron, so did the enemy change the magicians' rod into snakes. The difference, however, is that *God's* snake swallowed all of the magicians' snakes!

"Do not take your focus off *God*! That bird was not from *God*!" Grandma V stated firmly.

Just as the bat was swooping in closer, its feet turned to roots and it formed back to a tree.

Thump! it echoed as it collided with the ground.

"Is it gone?" Abby cried while peeking through the gaps between her fingers that were spread like a fan.

"Are you okay Abby?" Grandma hugged her.

"Yep, Grandma V," she squealed.

"Grandma V, I just can't do it," Zoey whined.

"You just need faith!" Grandma V informed with a smile.

CHAPTER 7

Most Christians are missing one vital component: belief in the supernatural. Now I know that doesn't include you! Otherwise, you would have never picked up this book!

Most people who lived in Oldsville were unaware that there were two different realms: the _natural realm_ and the _spiritual realm_. I know what you're thinking, what's the difference?

Well, the _natural realm_ consists of things that could be experienced through the five senses only: sight, touch, taste, smell, and hearing.

The _spiritual realm_ is also accessible; however, it's only revealed through the revelation of _God!_ For example, there are _spiritual_ beings all around, though people are only able to see them if their _spiritual eyes_ are opened!

There is a battle going on in both realms between good and evil. The Hartfords as well as other Anointeds were on the side of good! Now, let's see how things are going with Skylar and Zoey!

CHAPTER 8

FAITH IS THE KEY!

And Jesus said unto them, Because of your unbelief: for verily I say unto you, if ye have faith as a grain of mustard seed, ye shall say unto this mountain, remove hence to yonder place; and it shall remove; and nothing shall be impossible unto you.
(Mathew 17:20)

Grandma V turned to Zoey, "The key is to have faith, follow the Lord, and nothing will be impossible!"

Their grandma led them through a thick mist that overshadowed everything! The mist was so thick that they couldn't see their hands in front of their faces.

Skylar called out to her family. "Grandma V, Abby, Zoey!"

But no one answered her. Skylar wondered where everyone could be. She glanced to her left where Grandma V was just positioned. Then to her right where her sisters were. *Surely, they must be playing around,* she thought.

"Stop playing games!" Her tone revealed her uncertainty. In spite of her cries, there was no response.

Skylar wondered, *Should I go back?*

"No! I must have been too slow. Maybe if I run, I can catch up to them," she reasoned.

She stayed on the path and sped up a bit. Skylar continued to run in a straight line calling out their names ever so often. However, she got no response! She grew exhausted from running. Her vision was now obscured from the sweat trickling down her face. She had no idea where anyone could be; her situation seemed hopeless. Her frown slowly began to turn into a smile. *I know what I'll do, I've got to be closer now! I'll just call out again!* she thought.

"Hello?!" She used her shirt to wipe the sweat away. Skylar continued to call out! However, the only response she received was the continued echoes of her own voice beckoning back to her, "*hello, hello, hello.*"

Tears swelled up in her eyes. She made one last attempt to call out, "help!" as she sobbed. And again, she could only hear the continued echoes of her own voice. "*Help, help, help.*"

She took a deep breath in and exhaled forcefully. "Can anyone hear me?" she murmured. She wasn't really expecting to hear them respond. But this time there was *complete silence!* She noticed that the one sound she anticipated, *the echoes,* were silent as well! It chose not to make an appearance that time!

Skylar paused, "That's weird," as the wrinkle in her forehead deepened.

Skylar strangely felt comforted when she could actually hear the echoes of her voice. The presence of the silence confirmed a definite void, and that didn't comfort her at all!

Skylar began to nibble on her nails, as she often did whenever she was nervous.

"Okay, Skylar. Think logically," a smile crossed her face. "Grandma V would never put me in danger!"

She knew what she thought was true. However, she couldn't deny that the place became creepier with each passing moment. She noticed things she hadn't observed prior—like the dark trees overlapping one another. They appeared as if they were smiling at her, but in a *grimacing* manner! Not to mention the old, dark, and broken-down cottage off in the distance. It gave off a creepy feeling, as if something lived inside that was waiting to eat whatever came to the door!

"You're scaring yourself, Skylar! You can't be afraid! *God* has not given you the *spirit* of *fear*," she frantically shook her head from side to side.

Suddenly, Skylar was interrupted by subtle whispers.

"*sswswswsw.*" The sounds of whispers were nearby.

Skylar turned to her left and then to her right, but no one was there! Chills ran down her spine. "Hello? Grandma V? Zoey? Abby?" she squealed.

By the time she had gotten to Abby's name, there was a slight crack in her voice.

Then out of nowhere, a little man appeared! He was an older man and a little shorter than her. He had a gentle smile that was across his face as he hummed. He held an object that mirrored a flute. Skylar's initial reaction was relief. But then something felt *wrong*.

She was about to ask for help, but she hesitated for a moment. She pondered the possibility that even the enemy could come as an angel of light, thus appearing to be good! Suddenly, it was as if the little man believed that Skylar could *discern* his spirit and see his *true* heart.

With ease, his countenance began to shift. A vein pulsated in the corner of his head. His smile was now completely diminished, and his teeth were clenched together in anger. It took no time for the little man to charge full speed towards Skylar.

"I hate Anointeds!" he yelled as he catapulted forward.

Skylar knew that only one of them could win this battle. She didn't have time to cry, scream, or debate about what she needed to do. The little man was headed straight for her! She got on one knee and closed her eyes. "I pray that the enemy is removed now, in *Jesus Christ's* name!"

As Skylar spoke in faith, a shield appeared in front of her. The shield was the *Shield of Faith* from the *Armor of God!* Skylar's eyes were still closed as she prayed with faith!

Abby tugged on Grandma V's dress. Grandma V turned to Abby with her eyes beaming with pride!

"What is that?" Abby's eyes widened. "Grandma V do you see it?" Abby persisted with her line of questioning. "There is a shield in front of Skylar!"

The *Shield of Faith* was easily *seen* because they were in the *spiritual realm*! It glistened and shined with specs of gold all around it!

Grandma V and Abby could see Skylar, but she couldn't see them!

"Yes, sweetheart that is one of the *weapons of warfare* given to us by *God*! It's the *Shield of Faith*!" Grandma V pointed towards the shield.

"Oh wow, that's so cool!" Then Abby spun around in excitement.

Skylar cracked open one eye to see if her enemy was still there, but the four-foot man had *disappeared*! She stood to her feet and looked around to make sure he was really gone! She looked down and she noticed that she was holding the shield!

"Woah…" she said while almost fumbling it onto the ground. She took a moment to catch her breath. "Cool!"

The shield slowly faded away! Everything was quiet and still. Suddenly out of nowhere, the sound of applause erupted!

"Well done, my Skylar!" Grandma V cheered.

"Awesome! I didn't know you could do that Skylar," Abby expressed. She was proud of her big sister.

Skylar embraced them both! She was overjoyed to see them. "The *Word of God* just came to me, and I spoke what I needed to, and all the fear left!"

Grandma V pointed her finger at Skylar. "Your faith is very strong!"

"Grandma V, the *Shield of Faith* appeared!" Skylar said with excitement. Skylar's smile turned to a frown, "but as quickly as it appeared—it vanished!" She was afraid that she somehow lost the shield.

Grandma V lifted Skylar's chin up. "Don't worry sweetheart, it's still there."

A smile once again crossed Skylar's face.

"As long as you trust *God and* put on the armor—the shield will be there!" Grandma V explained.

And out of the corner of Skylar's eyes she could see a flicker of gold light, confirming what Grandma V said.

Skylar was proud of herself, but she couldn't help but miss Zoey's presence. Concern overwhelmed her; she couldn't celebrate her victory until she knew Zoey was alright.

"Grandma, where's Zoey?" She was now biting her nails once again.

Grandma V winked at Skylar and Abby. "She is caught in a mist, all her own."

****

Meanwhile, Zoey had done something very similar to her twin. She had called out to Grandma V several times. She swiftly came to the conclusion that this was some sort of test! She paused for a moment and stubbornly refused to go any further!

But the more she stood still, the louder the echoes of the animals in the forest became! She made the unfortunate decision to go in the opposite direction, which seemingly led her deeper and deeper into the forest.

"Grandma V, I know you have something up your sleeve." She rubbed the back of her head. "Fine I'll play along," she uttered disappointingly.

Zoey was annoyed. She was tired of walking and hated being alone! As she strolled deeper into the forest, she noticed an unusual looking flower off in the distance. The flower was beautiful, and its colors fluctuated constantly. It altered between the colors: red, green, and blue!

What an unusual flower, she thought as she bent down to pick it up.

"What are you doing here in this place? You're way too beautiful to be *here!*" Her gaze turned from the colorful flower to her gloomy surroundings.

Slowly, the mist was replaced by large droplets of rain. Zoey rubbed the raindrops from her eyes.

When her vision was clear, a four-foot-tall woman was skipping around picking some flowers as well. Like the man, she too appeared very pleasant. She smiled and waved at Zoey. Zoey felt relieved that she was no longer alone.

Maybe she knows where everyone is, Zoey considered.

She made her way over to the little woman. "Have you seen an older woman with two girls?"

The woman shook her head no. She smiled a genuine looking smile as she handed Zoey one of the flowers she had just picked.

Zoey held it to her nose and inhaled the beautiful scent of the flower. She waved goodbye to the woman and headed in the opposite direction. When she got about fifteen feet away, the woman screamed, "You Anointed!!" The woman too had a flute—like instrument in her hand.

Zoey had been deceived! When she smelled the flower, it released a toxin that made her *weak!* It made her so weak that she barely could lift her legs to run.

"What's wrong with my legs?" she cried. "Augh!" Zoey screamed as she attempted to run away from the woman.

But she felt as if she was moving in slow motion. She was expelling all her energy, but she wasn't going anywhere! Her legs now were heavy like bricks.

"Grandma V!!" she screamed, but no one answered.

"I'm going to get you! I hate Anointeds!!" The woman roared.

Zoey continued to run in slow motion, until she tripped on a branch lying on the ground. She glanced back and the woman was now only a few feet away.

"Help!!" Zoey cried. She regained strength, scrambled to her feet and started running once again. Out of nowhere, Grandma V appeared, and next to her stood Skylar and Abby!

Zoey's face was wet from a combination of raindrops and tears. She wiped the tears away and quickly took shelter behind Grandma V! Zoey slowly peeked from the side of Grandma V—but nothing was there!

Zoey began to yell. "Grandma V, it was a small woman chasing me with something!" She looked around. "Honestly, there was!"

Skylar and Abby laughed hysterically.

"You were so scared!!" Skylar held her stomach as if it was going to burst from laughter.

"Skylar didn't run away!" Abby giggled, "besides, I told you guys about talking to strangers!" She was being sarcastic.

Zoey's fear instantly turned to embarrassment and then...anger! She came to the realization that the woman was part of a test.

Grandma glanced at Abby and Skylar with a frown on her face. She was disappointed with them for making fun of

Zoey. She gently shook her head from side to side, chastising the girls for their behavior.

"Zoey, we know there was really someone chasing you. It was a test to reveal what level you girls were on. Those small people are called Javas. They're the ones I warned you about. They hate Anointeds and Mirans and anyone that's *good!* Their weapon of choice ironically looks like a flute, but it's so much more! It's called a shool.

"It has a red light that can freeze a person for a certain amount of time. Depending on the type of shool, the time varies how long the person will be frozen. The person is not aware of what's going on when the instrument is used. This is all they need to do to try and get the upper hand," she explained. "The shool is equipped with other features, I'm just not aware of all of them!"

Zoey twirled one strand of hair around her finger. "I wasn't afraid of the Java; I was only pretending," she insisted as she tugged on the strand of her hair, out of frustration.

"Sure you were." Skylar rolled her eyes.

"I was!" Zoey insisted once again as she stomped her feet on the ground.

Grandma V scolded Zoey. "Now you know lying is wrong!"

Grandma V had a way of correcting the girls in a loving manner yet still being firm. The same way the *Holy Spirit* corrects *Christians*—lovingly!

Zoey apologized to Grandma V for lying. She then looked at Grandma V with hopeful eyes. "So...did I pass?!"

Grandma V looked at Zoey with a confused look on her face. "You couldn't have possibly thought that the object of the lesson was to run away scared."

Skylar and Abby concealed their laughter. They wanted to avoid being chastised by Grandma V again.

"Well, Skylar, I bet you didn't pass either," Zoey shrieked with one eyebrow raised and a streak of confidence in her voice.

Skylar looked down on the ground to avoid eye contact with her sister. She knew she had done well, but she didn't want to make Zoey feel bad.

Abby broke the silence. "Skylar did great!"

Zoey eyeballed the ground. "Of course she did," she mumbled as she kicked the dust in the air. "Why wouldn't she?"

Grandma V walked over to Zoey and put her arms around her. "You girls will develop spiritually at your own pace. But you both are growing at such an alarming rate anyway! Just continue to exercise the *gift* and read the *word*. *God's* word is what encourages *spiritual growth*!" Grandma V exclaimed.

****

Everyone woke up one by one and they were back in the *natural realm*! With a yawn and a stretch, Abby began to jump up and down. "That was so much fun!"

They all entered the house and grabbed a bag full of cookies to take home with them.

"Now girls you can't mention this to your mom." Grandma V hated asking the girls to keep anything from their mom, but she knew that Hailey wouldn't understand. The girls sat in silence. "Trust me girls, this is what's best."

Grandma V looked down, with a longing look in her eyes. She hoped that her daughter had not moved too far away from *God*. Skylar and Zoey could see the pain in Grandma V's eyes. They embraced her.

"We understand, and we trust you. Don't worry we won't mention it," Skylar and Zoey replied. Grandma V had a relieved look on her face.

Skylar glanced out the window. "Grandma V, it's getting late! It's going to be dark by the time we get home!" Skylar had a panicked look on her face. "I don't like walking outside in the dark!" Zoey and Abby nodded their heads in agreement.

Grandma V closed her eyes, kneeled and silently prayed. She inquired of *God* with whom holds all power, to allow the sun to continue to shine! She could recall Joshua doing this in the midst of a battle.

And the sun stood still, and the moon stayed, until the people had avenged themselves upon their enemies. Is not this written in the book of Jasher? So the sun stood still in the midst of heaven, and hasted not to go down about a whole day.
(Joshua 10:13)

Suddenly the sun repositioned itself, and the moon moved back to its previous position.

"Girls, this will allow you a few hours to make it home before dark. Also, I've asked for a bus to come," and with a hug and a wave, Grandma V sent them on their way. The girls were amazed at the power of *God!*

CHAPTER 9

NARRATOR'S CORNER

*Finally, my brethren be strong in the Lord and
in the power of his might, Put on the whole
armour of God, that ye may be able to stand
against the wiles of the devil.
(Ephesians 6:10-11)*

*Grandma V just mentioned a little bit
about the armor of God to Abby!* Abby had
never heard of it, have you heard of the
armor of God? Christians are told to put on
the armor of *God* because their battle is not
natural—it's *spiritual!* This armor is similar
to what a knight would have worn around
the 8th century. The difference is this is a
spiritual armor, because the battle is
spiritual.

The armor consists of having your
loins equipped with the *truth*. And the

breastplate of *righteousness*. Having your feet shod with the *gospel of peace*. Putting on the helmet of *salvation*. And your sword is the sword of the *Spirit,* which is none other than the *Word of God!* And the shield which is the most important part of the armor, is a shield of *faith!* If you want to learn more about the armor of *God,* just read Ephesians 6:12-18!

There's one thing I can tell you, Skylar and Zoey were about to learn a whole lot about the *armor of God!*

CHAPTER 10

WELCOME BACK DAD!

The girls waved goodbye and headed to the bus stop. Rainn hid himself, making certain that he was nowhere near Grandma V's house. He patiently waited in the woods not too far from the bus stop. When the girls appeared, he inched his way on the bus as well. He ducked behind one of the seats so Zoey, Skylar, and Abby couldn't see him.

Once they arrived at their destination, Rainn tailed them as they got off the bus. He was tall and thin, so he easily hid behind street polls and trees.

Zoey was still a little disappointed because she didn't pass the test Grandma V gave her. Over and over in her mind she wondered how her twin could think of what to do so quickly!

She always felt like Skylar was smarter and braver than her in some instances, though, she would never admit that to anyone! The majority of the time, she had a hard time admitting it to herself.

Skylar didn't like the silence; it made her uncomfortable. She pondered on a subject that could lighten the mood. "I didn't know Grandma V could speak to *God.*"

"Grandma V isn't the only one keeping secrets!" Zoey murmured as she rolled her eyes and folded her arms.

Skylar felt that it was unfair for her to feel bad for passing the test. But, for some reason, she did! Deep inside, she wished that she had not done as well as she did, so that Zoey wouldn't feel like a failure. She couldn't understand why her sister would put so much pressure on herself, but Zoey had always been that way!

* * * * * * * * *

Rainn dodged back and forth behind cars, he leaped behind trees and even wooden fences. He made sure that he kept enough distance so that the girls wouldn't see him. After all, he just met them and didn't want to frighten them.

So, their mother is an Anointed and their father is a Miran. How interesting! Rainn thought.

Skylar stopped and turned around; she could *sense* that someone was there.

Rainn bent his knees and leaped into the bushes. He knew that Grandma V would be extremely upset if she knew he had stuck around. In spite of his fear of Grandma V, he wanted to ensure that the girls got home safely.

Skylar turned around. Her eyes were squinted. Zoey was walking ahead of Skylar with Abby right beside her. Abby had managed to turn Zoey's attention on something less stressful—her plans for the summer!

Abby pulled Zoey's arm so she would stop walking and turn her focus on Skylar.

Zoey made her way back to Skylar. She tilted her head to the right and repositioned her body in front of her sister to obscure her view. "What's wrong, Skylar?"

Skylar stood silent. She hadn't heard Zoey at all; she just continued to stare.

"Well, are you going to tell me what's wrong?!" Zoey demanded.

Skylar didn't know what she was feeling or why. She shrugged her shoulders and continued walking. "Never mind."

Rainn wiped the sweat from his brow. "That was close," he admitted while releasing a sigh.

****

The girls were standing in front of their Victorian home. The home was two stories. It had a brick front with red shutters, and a large wrap-around porch. The twins had spent many days playing there, when the weather didn't permit them to play in the yard.

They enjoyed the rocking chairs and running under the steps in one of their many ventures of cops and robbers!

Skylar was imagining Grandma V rocking back and forth like she always did when she used to visit more often. Unfortunately, their mom and Grandma V didn't see eye to eye on many things. However, the area they butted heads on the most was unfortunately about *God*.

Their home had an old wooden swing tied to a tree in the front yard. The tree's branches were partially leaned over due to the girls climbing and pulling on the swing over the years. Abby leaped on the swing and began kicking her legs high in the air.

When Zoey and Skylar headed into the house. Skylar saw Zoey sulking; her focus went back on what her sister hinted at earlier.

"Zoey, it's not a big deal, and I'm not keeping secrets. I just wasn't frightened," Skylar paused. "Well, I mean, I was afraid, but it went away! I don't know why," Skylar admitted as she grabbed an apple.

Zoey slammed her bookbag on the kitchen table. "Yeah, whatever!"

Abby leaped off the swing and joined her big sisters in the house.

"That was so much fun! I want to stay at Grandma Vs for the summer!" Abby shouted while jumping up and down.

Skylar and Zoey's eyebrows rose. They each grabbed one of Abby's arms.

"Have a seat, Abby." They sat their sister down in a chair at the kitchen table. They both kneeled down in order to be eye to eye with her. "You can't mention anything to Mom about today," they both informed, "Okay?"

Abby's excitement quickly diminished, "I know… I know…" she murmured as she laid back in the chair while kicking her feet in disappointment. "I hate keeping secrets from Mom."

"We know. We hate it too, but if it was anyone besides Grandma V asking, we wouldn't keep the secret from her. But Grandma V needs our help!" Skylar retorted.

Abby didn't respond, she just sat in her seat picking over a sandwich that Zoey pulled out of the refrigerator for her.

"This is serious Abby, no jokes. Mom won't let us go to Grandma V's, at all this summer if you slip up!" Zoey stated firmly.

Abby sighed deeply. "I won't say anything," she mumbled disappointingly.

They knew the only reason Grandma V asked them to keep quiet was because their mom wouldn't understand. Her lack of understanding could greatly interfere with whatever they were preparing for. Their mom had loved *God* as a child but when she began to distance herself from him, it was as if she no longer understood *spiritual* things.

But the natural man receiveth not the things of the Spirit of God, for they are foolishness unto him: neither can he know them, because they are spiritually discerned.

(1 Corinthians 2:14)

When a person becomes more concerned with worldly things, rather than the things of *God*, it's harder for them to understand *Spiritual* things.

Just then, the screen door on the porch slammed, "Hey girls!" their dad called.

"Dad!" screams of joy overtook the room.

Dad picked all three of his daughters up at once and spun them around in a circle and placed them down. He then rubbed his speckled beard on their faces! The girls loved the way it tickled their cheeks.

"It sure is good to come home to a house full of princesses! I missed you so much!" he smiled.

"Dad, how was U-rope?" Abby inquired.

"Europe! Silly!" Zoey rustled the top of Abby's hair.

Dad snickered. "Well, it's beautiful, I'm sure. But my job kept me in a stuffy office. Maybe one day soon we can take a family trip there."

"That would be great! Then when Lizzy asks, I can finally say, yes—we've been out the country!" Skylar joked.

Everyone giggled.

"Grandma V can probably snap her fingers and have the whole family there," Zoey jokingly implied.

Abby's eyes got big. She grabbed her dad's briefcase. "Grandma V could do it with no problem. Why just today she—"

Before Abby could finish, Skylar covered her mouth.

"What did you say, baby girl?" Dad asked.

"You know Abby, she's always mumbling about something," Zoey replied.

Skylar shooed Abby out of the room.

Abby covered her own mouth for two reasons: as a means of disciplining herself and to ensure she wouldn't slip up again!

Dad saw the back of Abby's ponytail turning the corner as she sprinted up the stairs.

"You girls know how your mother feels about talking about *Spiritual things* when Abby's in the room," he pointed out with a disappointed look on his face.

"Dad, can I ask you a question?" Zoey asked.

"Sure," Dad loosened his tie.

"Do you ever miss it? You know, operating in gifts and stuff?"

It was as if mentioning it brought back wonderful memories that their dad hadn't thought of for many years! The truth was, he had grown accustomed to his *regular* life, yet there was something that was still missing.

He loved when he had a personal relationship with *Jesus Christ*, worshipping the *Father*, and hearing the *Holy Spirit!* He also craved to see miracles again and operate in the *Gifts of the Spirit*. But he knew that he had to make a choice. So, he chose their mom. But at the time he didn't realize that it would *completely* interfere with his relationship with *God!*

"Gifts, gifts, gifts...Doesn't anyone talk about anything else?" Mom whined, as she toddled Nick in one hand and two bags of groceries in the other.

"Well, hello beautiful. Rough day I presume?" Dad placed a kiss on Mom's cheek and graciously relieved her of Nick.

"Hey, big boy!" he shouted while spinning Nick around.

"Dad!" Nick squealed excitedly.

"Well Dad, do you miss being a *real* Christian?" Zoey inquired.

"Maybe we'll talk about this another time sweetheart." Their dad avoided the question, because he knew it was a sensitive topic for his wife.

"Why, Aden? Just answer the question. Nothing like the present—right?" Mom had one eyebrow raised out of curiosity.

Their dad knew where this was going. If he revealed that he missed it, Mom would feel guilty for influencing such a change in him. If he lied and stated that he didn't miss it, then she would feel that there was nothing wrong and that stepping away from *God* was no big deal… And Dad knew that wasn't true!

Dad hesitated for a moment; he pondered on what his response would mean—not only to his family but to *God* as well! Dad knew that he needed to choose wisely! He looked at his two *little girls* staring up at him, waiting, and anticipating his response. And on the other side was Hailey, standing impatiently, tapping her nails on the counter, in hopes of swaying his decision in her direction!

Out of nowhere, there was a knock at the back door.

"I'll get it!" Dad shouted with relief over his face as he breezed past their mom to get the door.

It was their neighbor, Mr. Fico. He was a tall man with a broad build. He had short black hair and smooth skin. He stood there with his clean-shaven face and sparkling white teeth. Mr. Fico's eyes were unusual. They were soft and peaceful and as blue as the deep blue sea!

"Hey, Aden. I sure do hate to be a bother. But I have been trying to start my lawnmower for the better part of an hour and I haven't had any luck." Mr. Fico stood in the doorway and pointed towards his lawnmower sitting in his driveway.

He removed his baseball cap and scratched the top of his head. "So, I thought to myself... *self*, that limo just dropped Aden off. Being the handy man that you are, I figured I'd come on by and have you get this bad boy started before it gets too late to cut the grass!"

Dad breathed a sigh of relief! He placed Nick down and hurried Mr. Fico out the door. "What are neighbors for?" Dad declared as he followed Mr. Fico outside.

It was as if Mr. Fico *knew* that Aden needed someone to *rescue* him.

Mom began to unpack the groceries. "Where is Abby?"

"She's upstairs playing," Skylar replied.

"Why don't you girls go outside and play? After all, it is officially summer break, and it'll be dark soon!"

Through all the excitement of being with Grandma V, the girls had forgotten all about the start of summer!

Abby came sliding down the stairs on her bottom. "I thought I heard your voice, Mom!" She ran up and hugged her.

"Hey, buttercup! Grab your shoes because the girls are taking you outside to play!"

****

Dad had just got done repairing Mr. Fico's lawnmower.

Boy, that was a close one, he thought while tightening the screws.

"Is it fixed?" Mr. Fico inquired.

Dad stood up and brushed the dust off his pants, "of course," with a snicker and a gleam of pride in his eyes.

"Well, that's about two million dollars I owe you, huh?" Mr. Fico joked while stepping back to admire the lawn-mower.

Zoey, Abby, and Skylar were playing in the driveway. Abby was riding around on her new tricycle, Zoey was bouncing around a basketball, and Skylar was tying her roller skates.

Skylar and Zoey's best friend Steph-anie was coming down the street with her poodle. They met Stephanie when she first came to Oldsville Terrace and rode their school bus. At first, she appeared like any other child. She had chubby cheeks with deep dimples and long, sandy, blonde hair.

Stephanie would always wear plaid skirts and button-down shirts with dress sh-oes. Her attire met Skylar's approval! The girls always assumed it was because she came from a private school, but neither of the twins dared to ask. It took no time for the other children to poke fun at the way she dressed.

But the girls quickly learned that th-ere was something *special* about Stephanie.

It didn't matter what insults the other kids hurled in Stephanie's direction, she would smile and behave as if no one said a word. The girls soon found that the reason Stephanie had so much confidence was because she had a friend that was greater than any friend she could ever hope to have in school! She had a friend in *JESUS*!

She not only believed in *Jesus* she understood that *He* was the role model for every Christian! *Jesus* exudes love and patience, and Stephanie knew that as a Christian, she was called to do the same thing!

The girls admired her strength! In no time, they realized that all three of them shared this mutual *friend*, and in return, *their* friendship blossomed! Now many years later, Stephanie's style has deviated a bit, but her relationship with *Jesus* has only grown stronger and so has her relationship with Zoey and Skylar!

"Hey, Steph!" Skylar held on to the garage door in order to assist her with balancing on her skates.

"Hey guys! I didn't see you two on the bus ride home. What happened?" Stephanie blew a bubble with her bubble gum.

Zoey peeked over at Skylar and shrugged her shoulders in a nonchalant manner.

Why not tell Stephanie, it's not like we could get in trouble with her? they both thought.

"We went to our grandma's house," Zoey said while tossing the ball at Stephanie.

"What? Doesn't she live far, like out in the country!" Stephanie squealed with concern.

Dad overheard Zoey. *I hope Mom doesn't find out, she wouldn't be too happy* he thought to himself.

"Not so loud!" Skylar whispered as she walked closer to Stephanie.

"Oh, sorry!" Stephanie replied. She covered her mouth with her hands and inadvertently dropped her poodle's leash.

Just then, Roxy, Stephanie's poodle, saw her opportunity to take off running! She darted out into the street.

"Oh no!" Stephanie screamed.

"Stay here!" Skylar yelled to Abby while pointing firmly.

Zoey and Stephanie ran down the street following Roxy. Stephanie's mom always told her to never let Roxy's leash go. Stephanie felt awful! Skylar desperately tried to keep up, despite her not being a good skater!

"Stop Roxy!" Stephanie hollered.

CHAPTER 11

THE NEW NEIGHBORS!

Roxy was running back and forth under cars, around trash cans, and leaping over fire hydrants. Roxy was running fast and she periodically glanced back to make sure the girls weren't gaining any ground! They finally had her cornered at the end of a cul-de-sac.

"Don't worry, Stephanie! She doesn't have anywhere to go!" Zoey reassured as she leaned over and gasped for air.

Suddenly a car pulled out of the driveway of a house at the end of the cul-de-sac, but Roxy was going full speed ahead and was headed straight for the car!

"I can't look!" Stephanie screamed as she shielded her eyes and turned her head.

Zoey silently prayed, and the sounds of children playing, the car tires squealing, and Stephanie screaming faded in the background! All movement ceased; even the clouds halted. But more importantly, the car stopped!

Skylar finally caught up with them.

"What happened to everyone?" she asked while tapping Stephanie's head with her knuckles. "She's frozen! Everyone's frozen except us! How did you do that?"

Zoey had already gone over and picked Roxy up—who, by the way, looked like nothing more than a porcelain doll!

"Did you hear me?" Skylar's voice was mixed with frustration and curiosity at the same time.

"Yes, I heard you. I guess you're not the only one holding on to little secrets," Zoey snickered.

The truth was, Zoey didn't do anything. She asked *God* to intervene, and *He* did! Just as if time never stopped, everything went back to normal.

Stephanie was still shielding her eyes and sobbing.

"Don't sweat, Steph. Here is your pet!" Zoey lowered Stephanie's hands from her face.

"Roxy!" Stephanie grabbed her poodle and began kissing her. "How? Never mind who cares?"

Zoey and Skylar winked at each other.

"Get out of the street!" The man hollered as he drove off.

"Sorry Mister!" The girls yelled.

They didn't notice the young girl that was about their age standing in her yard. She was waving goodbye to the man in the car.

Stephanie was staring at the house. She remembered the stories of a man that used to live there. Rumor had it, balls would roll in his yard, and he would *eat* them!

"Hey, isn't this the house Old Man Finny lived in?" Stephanie asked.

Stephanie always tried to speak low when she was supposed to be whispering, but she was rarely successful at the task! Her *quiet* voice was the same tone as her *normal* one. One would venture to say it was a tad bit louder!

Skylar turned to face the home. She observed that the new buyers still kept the front door painted black! *How odd!* she thought. Mr. Finny painted that door black many years ago. The HOA, along with other neighbors, were outraged but no one dared to confront him! After all, he wasn't the nicest person.

Everyone seemed to avoid him at all costs! Skylar saw bushes that were overrun due to it not being trimmed, and the grass was at least a foot high! Skylar shook her head. *The house looks exactly the same. The new owners must have taken a page out of Mr. Finny's book,* she thought.

"Yeah, this is the house. I didn't know that he finally sold it." Skylar looked around with a slight wrinkle on her nose.

"Me neither. You know, the old legends say that the house has been haunted since the late 1800s," Stephanie replied while winding Roxy's leash nice and tight around her wrist.

Zoey and Skylar didn't believe in the haunted stories, but they always had a feeling of heaviness whenever they were near the home.

"Heck, I didn't know this neighborhood was that old." Zoey felt a slight shiver go down her spine.

"They say that every family that's lived in that house—has turned evil." Stephanie emphasized the word *evil*.

The girls stood silently, looking at the windows that were extremely narrow. The front door had an uncanny resemblance to a mouth opening wide. The porch was old, and the banister was badly in need of a fresh coat of paint. Even the big pecan tree that was growing in the front yard had a hint of creepiness (if you will) as it leaned over from the weight of the nuts on its branches.

The girls each stood staring at the house with their own horrifying expressions. Grateful no doubt that none of them had to live there!

A young girl approached them from behind. "You gonna stand there telling fictional stories about my house or are you gonna introduce yourselves?" The girl asked in an annoyed tone.

The girls were all startled and jumped simultaneously.

The girl had a smug look on her face and shrugged her shoulders. "Your own ghost stories have got you girls scared, huh?" She swiped her trimmed bangs out of her face. She had smooth, flawless skin, almost like a model. Her hair was sandy brown, and she wore jean shorts and an old t-shirt that read, *If you can read this, you've been looking way too long.* She had dark brown eyes. She was about average height. The girl's confidence was evident, and she spoke slow and steady.

She observed the girls as if she was in Biology class dissecting a frog. She continued. "I'm Alexia, Alexia McClaire, and that was my dad pulling out of the driveway. I'm so glad your dog didn't get run over." Her steady eyes were fixated on Roxy, "For a moment it looked like she was toast! Funny thing though—next thing I saw, you were holding her." She turned and pointed to Zoey.

"I thought the exact same thing!" Stephanie interrupted with a grateful smile, "lucky me!"

"Yeah, lucky you!" Zoey took a moment to silently thank *God* once more.

Alexia stared at Zoey with her brown eyes laser focused on her.

Skylar nudged past Stephanie. She knew that she needed to change the subject before Alexia became too suspicious.

"I'm Skylar. This is my sister Zoey and our best friend Stephanie.

Alexia's attention turned to Skylar. "Nice to meet all of you." She extended her hand.

Alexia looked back at her home. "I know it's not much," she shrugged her shoulders, "but I like to think it has character!"

Stephanie, Zoey, and Skylar felt bad for speaking negatively about Alexia's house. They immediately began to speak at once. "Yeah, sure! Of course!"

Alexia paused for a moment and once again began to examine the girls. There was awkward silence for the span of about seven seconds.

"Do you have any sisters or brothers?" Stephanie asked as she brushed Roxy's coat.

Skylar and Zoey were grateful for a break in the silence.

Alexia awkwardly paused for a second more and then responded. "As a matter of fact, I do."

Stephanie smiled. "What are their ages?"

"Well, I'm eleven and my sisters are five, nine, and twelve, and I have a brother who is sixteen. We just moved here from Maine. We haven't been here long, but this seems like a pretty quiet little town." She took a moment to take in the scenery around her.

Zoey was studying Alexia as well. It was something odd about Alexia, but she just couldn't quite put her finger on it!

As Alexia spoke about her sisters, she was suddenly reminded that Abby was waiting on them—alone! "Well, it was nice to meet you Alexia, but speaking of sisters, we left ours in the driveway by herself!" The girls waved goodbye and ran towards the house.

"Mom is going to kill us!" Skylar yelled as she skated closely behind the others.

Alexia watched the girls until they were mere specs off in the distance. A crooked smile crossed her face and in a creepy tone, she demanded, "show yourselves!"

Alexia's three sisters, one by one, became visible! They were there all along, listening and watching the girls. They had mastered the art of being hidden in plain sight and were guilty of using that strategy quite often.

The oldest sister's name was Chloe. She had long, stringy brown hair and a pale complexion. Chloe rolled her shoulders and cracked her neck from side to side. She was the muscle of the group, *if you will*.

She was short-tempered and the first to jump at the opportunity to take part in a brawl, even when she wasn't personally involved in the conflict! Chloe had proven to be quite an asset to her family! She was tall for being only twelve. She stood at 5'6, and she was often dubbed the *tomboy* of the group! She embraced the title.

"Well, I think these are the Anointeds we've been looking for!" Alexia said.

Chloe groaned. "Well, what are we waiting for?" she said while charging ahead.

"Wait!" Alexia pulled Chloe's shirt to keep her from walking off. "We have to be smart about this! We have to befriend them and gain their trust. Besides, with them together and without a plan—they're much too strong!"

"Too strong for who?" Chloe pounded her fist in her hand.

Alexia's five-year-old sister was sitting crisscross in midair playing with a hideous-looking doll. "They don't look so tough to me! I can take them by myself!" she hissed.

Tammy admired Chloe's strength and wanted to be *just* like her. She began to pound her fists together (imitating Chloe) as hard as she could. She always looked for an opportunity to impress her big sister. The only problem was that Tammy pounded her fist a little too hard. "Ouch!" she whined.

Tammy had two pigtails in her hair, brown eyes, and a small scar over her left eye from wielding a tree branch a little too closely.

Their mother stepped outside and motioned for the girls to come in. Once inside, they took their usual places around the room. Tammy sat crisscross in midair, Alexia was on the couch, Chloe was leaning against the wall nearby, and ten-year-old Rhonda was sitting quietly in a chair with a book on her lap.

Rhonda had hair to the middle of her back. Her hair was soft, curly, and black with brown streaks. She was a little small for her age and had a gentleness about her *unlike the others*. She was the spitting image of her mother, but her personality couldn't be more different.

Their mother's name was Lucinda McClaire. She never allowed the girls to call her *mother* for some reason, only their half-brother Austin was allowed to. Although they didn't understand why, they did as they were told. They dared not challenge Lucinda McClaire!

Lucinda McClaire had long hair the color of midnight, that reached to the middle of her back as well. Her nails were about an inch and a half in length and her skin was as smooth as a baby's bottom. Although she had outward beauty, on the inside she was as rotten as a year-old apple! She permeated darkness, and the sound of her voice was eerie.

She spoke slow and calculative, and her voice carried an authoritative tone! As sinister as her voice was, her eyes were even stranger. Looking into her eyes was like staring into nothing...It was empty!

She stood in the middle of the room near the fireplace. "Now girls, we have been sent to this sleepy town to eliminate the Hartfords and all of you have passed the first test...*identifying them*!" She gazed around the room and slowly clapped her hands together to offer a lazy, forced round of applause! Alexia, Chloe, Rhonda, and Tammy all looked on with enthusiasm. They appreciated the *slightest* hint of Lucinda McClaire's approval!

She swiftly adjusted her posture, revealing that she was clearly uncomfortable with displaying any form of affection. She placed her hands on her hips and continued. "I would have never guessed that an Anointed would make themselves known in front of everyone! She showed her ability to freeze time. Which brings me to you, Tammy!" Her cold eyes stared into Tammy's.

"I know your powers are new, but you can't sit in midair outside!" Lucinda McClaire scolded while continuing to stare. Tammy's attempt to hide her fear didn't last. Her feelings betrayed her as she began to visibly shake. Tammy put her head down and floated back to the floor.

There was a quiver in her voice. "Sorry, Lucinda McClaire."

Lucinda McClaire smiled with satisfaction after scolding Tammy as if she was victorious in some sort of battle!

"Which brings me to my second point; you girls need to live, look, and behave like other children! Both indoors and out!"

Chloe and Tammy joined Alexia on the couch. Lucinda McClaire walked over to Rhonda and grabbed her book. She rolled her eyes and tossed it in the fireplace!

Rhonda leaned back in her chair with her eyes wide.

"What do you need with books? You're a McClaire!" she scolded. She turned her attention back to the other girls, "And Alexia is right. The twins are too powerful together. No matter how tough you girls are, they are twice as dangerous and twice as powerful. I don't even think they know the extent of their power!" She tapped her nails on the coffee table over and over, with a creepy smile across her face. "We can use that to our advantage. We have to outwit them."

Alexia wondered how Lucinda Mc-Claire knew about the conversation she had with her sisters outside. Lucinda McClaire had a habit of—knowing things. Truth was the girls were *taught* to hide in plain sight by Lucinda McClaire. So, there should have been no surprise that Lucinda McClaire could do the same!

"Mother!" their brother yelled as he entered the room with a sub sandwich in his hand.

"Hi, Austin, have you had enough to eat?" Lucinda asked as she tapped his baseball cap.

"Yep. I'm going to go outside and play some baseball!" Austin balanced his sandwich in one hand and the ball and glove in the other as he left to go outside.

Their mother glanced through the window and watched Austin tossing the ball up in the air and catching it with the glove. He was headed to the park.

Their mother continued. "Remember girls, Austin doesn't know what our mission is."

Austin had the same father as the neighbors but a different mother. Austin and their dad were nothing like Lucinda McClaire and her daughters.

"He's not a Hazil like us. He mustn't ever know anything!" she warned. "Neither of them!" she added as her voice echoed throughout the house.

****

When the girls got back to the house, Abby was still playing in the driveway.

"What a good girl," Skylar confirmed as she picked her up.

"Girls, come on in and eat!" Mom yelled as she flung the screen door open.

"Just in the nick of time!" Zoey replied as they gave each other a high five.

Stephanie waved goodbye as her and Roxy headed home.

CHAPTER 12

AN UNEXPECTED SURPRISE!

The first official day of summer was full of sunshine, flowers blooming, and birds chirping outside. A ray of light shined through the corners of the blinds and directly into Skylar's eyes. She sat up in bed and did a long stretch.

She jumped up and down on Zoey's bed and hollered, "it's the first official day of summer!"

"Go away, Skylar," she whined as she opened one eye to peek at the clock. She continued, "you've got to be kidding me! It's only 7:00 am! Why are you up so early? As you just acknowledged, *it is summer!*" Zoey said in a groggy voice.

Skylar had a burst of energy. She jumped off the bed and began to pretend she was sword fighting in midair.

She ran and opened her bathroom door, which happened to be connected to their room and closed it quickly behind her. Zoey rolled over and pulled the covers over her head. The shuffle of little feet entered the room.

Go away, Zoey thought as she gripped the covers even tighter. Abby looked around the room and saw that Skylar wasn't in her bed. She saw Zoey laying down, trying to be as still as possible. Zoey hoped that her pretending to sleep would make Abby go away.

Abby thought this would be a good time to be naughty. She tiptoed across the room and took a good grip of Zoey's sheets. She tugged at the sheets with all the strength a five-year-old could muster. It was as if Zoey already knew what Abby was planning, and she pulled the covers back in the opposite direction, which resulted in Abby flying forward onto Zoey's bed.

"Please, Zoey!" she whined as she tried one more time but failed to move the covers. Abby decided to give up and moved slowly towards the door.

Zoey could hear the shuffle of Abby's feet moving away. She figured since her sisters obviously were not going to allow her to sleep in, someone needed to pay! She crept behind Abby and grabbed her little sister's shoulders.

"Ah!" Abby screamed.

Abby yelled so loudly that Skylar came running out of the bathroom with a mouth full of toothpaste. "What's going on!" she yelled in a panicked voice.

Abby was standing there silently, still a little shaken up.

Skylar glanced at Zoey who, by the way, was laughing hysterically.

"Stop scaring her Zoey!" Skylar wiped the toothpaste from around her mouth.

Zoey leaped back into bed and rolled over with her eyes squinted. "I'm not scaring anyone! I'M TRYING TO SLEEP!" she joked.

Skylar ignored Zoey. "Are Mom and Dad here?"

"Mom left early with Nick, remember? He has a doctor's appointment. I think Dad is getting ready for work. Are we still having a babysitter this summer now that Mom is working again?" Abby asked.

Skylar didn't respond because she wasn't sure. But Skylar had a sneaky suspicion that the babysitter may be coming sooner than they expected.

"I hope not!" Zoey yelled from beneath the sheets.

"Come on little one, let's get you some cereal," Skylar replied while purposely changing the subject.

****

Abby was sitting on the barstool, spinning around in a circle as fast as her little arms would allow her to go, as she watched cartoons. Skylar placed Abby's cereal in front of her.

"Not so fast, little one. You're going to make yourself dizzy." Skylar quickly grabbed Abby's chair—forcing it to stop spinning.

"Okay," Abby said disappointingly as she began to eat.

Zoey came into the kitchen fully dressed and made her way over to the window and opened the blinds and curtains.

"Hey!" Abby and Skylar yelled while holding up their hands to block the sun from their eyes.

"It's too bright!" Skylar squealed.

"Oh no, you two wanted to wake me up! So, here's a little Vitamin D with your cereal!" Zoey smirked while walking over to the refrigerator and grabbing an apple.

Dad walked in the kitchen. "You girls play nice today," he said as he grabbed his briefcase in one hand and an orange in the other.

"Don't we always?" Skylar replied with a half-smile.

He waved goodbye and walked out the door.

For a moment, Zoey and Abby did a victory dance. They were excited by the possibility that they may not get a babysitter after all!

A few moments later, there was a knock at the door. Their excitement quickly diminished.

Now Skylar had the definite answer to Abby's question. "We must be having a baby-sitter after all." Skylar opened the door.

Standing on the porch was a tall slender woman with blue eyes. Her hair was blonde, and she had shoulder length hair. She was wearing a black skirt with red heels and a burgundy blouse. She was dressed as if she was going to a job interview.

She had debated earlier that morning on what she should wear. She was more comfortable in jeans and a T-shirt and her favorite pair of baby blue sneakers, but she figured she should make a good first impression! After all, this was a job, and it was only her first day.

But this wasn't just any job. She had to get it! She was on *assignment* and not being hired was not an option! She knew all about the girls and their family and she knew she was sent to help them! Skylar and Zoey weren't aware that she was an *Anointed* as well, but her assignment was different from theirs. There were many *Anointeds*, however, they had different callings.

She stood there, twirling a yellow umbrella (which matched the color of her hair) in one hand and a sack in the other.

Skylar thought to herself how strange it was that the woman had an umbrella and there wasn't a cloud in the sky!

"Hello sweetheart, my name is Cassey Cain, but you can call me Miss CC," she insisted with a gentle smile.

She maneuvered her way towards Abby, "you must be Abby!" while pinching her cheeks. "You're even cuter than I imagined," she admitted with a wink.

Zoey peered at the lady and continued eating her breakfast as if Miss CC wasn't there. She had hoped that they had somehow changed their parents' minds about having a babysitter. But she now knew that their decision was final.

"And are you Skylar or Zoey?" Miss CC inquired as she turned to Skylar.

She felt that between the twins, the one that opened the door seemed a lot more pleasant.

"I'm Skylar, and that's Zoey," Skylar threw Miss CC a welcoming smile.

Zoey rolled her eyes as she tossed the rest of her apple in the trash.

Miss CC thought it best to initially be professional with the girls. She shook Skylar's hand, "nice to meet you," and handed her and Abby a large lollipop.

The girls' eyes lit up!

"Wow! I didn't know they made lollipops this big! It's got to be at least a foot wide!" Skylar ripped the plastic off.

"Cool! A lollipop first thing after breakfast!" Abby winked at Miss CC. "you're my kind of babysitter!"

Miss CC giggled.

Zoey glanced over and thought to herself, *If she thinks I'm some little kid that can be bought with a lollipop, she's got another thing coming!*

Miss CC looked over at Zoey; she knew that Zoey wasn't going to be won over so easily.

She cautiously made her way over to Zoey and extended her hand.

Zoey folded her arms.

"Okay." Miss CC took a deep breath and gazed up at the ceiling. "Well, would you like a lollipop at least?" she eased the lollipop across the counter towards Zoey.

"No!" Zoey's tone carried a hint of aggravation.

She slid the lollipop back towards Miss CC, but deep down inside, she really wanted it! However, she felt that taking it was a form of surrender! She could hear her sisters off in the distance bragging about the cotton candy and infused berry flavors of the lollipops!

Cotton candy flavor infused with berries! I've never heard of that before! Zoey thought to herself. But she stubbornly stood her ground—no way she would give in! She wasn't ready to wave her white flag just yet!

Miss CC was the enemy...after all, she was—*the Babysitter!*

Miss CC was sitting on the stool across from Zoey. "Zoey, it's quite obvious that you don't want me here. But I promise once you get to know me, you'll fall in love." Her voice made a slight elevation when she emphasized the word *love.*

She reached her hand forward to hold Zoey's, but Zoey stood up and ran upstairs.

Miss CC managed to plaster a smile on her face, in spite of her feeling defeated. She watched as Skylar and Abby danced around the room holding their lollipops. She decided to focus on the two girls who were happy to have her around. "Well girls, I have so much fun planned for you today." She tried to make her voice sound excited.

Miss CC paused for a moment and realized that she hadn't met their parents yet, not officially that is! She spoke with their mom on the phone. She knew that some strings were pulled for her to get this opportunity. After all, she came highly recommended, but she was still a little confused.

"Are your parents here to interview me? I mean, I spoke to your mom over the phone but—"

"No, they both already left! But for you to be here *alone* with us means only one thing: our mom has done a thorough background check on you," Skylar said between licks.

"Oh...ok." Miss CC realized that *God* must have been involved in her getting hired without an in-person interview!

"Please excuse me, Miss CC." Skylar headed upstairs to check on Zoey.

When she entered the room, Zoey was lying across the bed on her stomach. She was kicking her legs back and forth vigorously.

"What's wrong?" Skylar's forehead was wrinkled.

"I don't understand why we didn't go to Grandma V's house for the summer now that Mom's working! Why do we have to stay here with a boring babysitter?"

"I don't know. But what I do know is that with that attitude, Mom won't be letting us do much of anything this summer," Skylar mumbled.

Just then, Miss CC and Abby entered the room.

"Girls, we are going to have so much fun today! What would you like to do: go outside and play, go to the pool, or maybe even go to the park?" Miss CC clasped her hands together in excitement. She was hoping that a little fun would change Zoey's mood.

"Let's go to the pool today!" Abby screamed while purposely waiting for no input from her sisters. She ran into her room to put on her bathing suit.

Miss CC made her way over to Zoey's bed. It just didn't sit right with her that one of the girls was upset! It was easy for her to identify which one was Zoey, after all she was the one that was pouting.

She leaned in closer and placed her palm on Zoey's leg. "I know how you feel Zoey. You think you're too big to have a babysitter. I remember feeling the same way when I was a little girl!" Zoey perked up a bit.

Miss CC continued. "My parents never wanted me to be alone, so they gave me a friend, it was a brown dog. His name was Rusty, and he went everywhere with me!" Miss CC circled the room and faced Zoey with a huge smile. "He was great! When I became an adult, I got another friend and now I'm giving him to you!"

Miss CC reached behind her back and pulled out a rabbit! It wasn't just an average rabbit; this rabbit was the color of a candy bar! Then it turned caramel and then fiery red with gray stripes! It was now avocado green and milky white!

Skylar and Zoey watched in amazement! They couldn't believe how this rabbit could change colors on a whim!

Zoey jumped to her feet and ran up to Miss CC. "Wow! She's beautiful!"

"Excuse me! Handsome would be more appropriate!" The rabbit snared as he shook strands of Miss CC's blonde hair off him.

They jumped back!

"Girls, you don't have to be afraid. He won't hurt you!"

Miss CC knew they had a million questions running through their little heads, so she began to answer them as if she were reading their minds. "Yes, he is a rabbit—yes, he can talk—yes I am absolutely giving him to you!" She handed him to Zoey.

Zoey hesitated for a moment and then she took the rabbit and embraced him.

Their faces turned from fear to excitement!

Miss CC leaned in closer and whispered. "Now girls, this is our little secret."

Skylar and Zoey nodded their heads in agreement with large smiles across their faces.

"Hi, I'm Oliver," the rabbit said.

The girls introduced themselves as well.

"How is it that he can talk?" Skylar tilted her head to the right in disbelief.

In spite of Oliver being able to speak, they couldn't help but direct all their questions towards Miss CC.

"Well, there are many animals that can talk!" Miss CC replied.

The girls weren't aware that animals could speak, but they did remember the story in the *Bible* about the donkey speaking in the book of Numbers 22:21-35.

"A talking rabbit! Wow! Now that's cool!" Abby was standing by the door watching.

"It's supernatural!" Abby yelled.

Miss CC leaned in towards Abby. "And what exactly do you know about *supernatural* things?" she probed.

"Well—" before Abby could finish, Skylar changed the subject.

"This is incredible!" she said while touching the rabbit's head.

Skylar didn't want to say anything to Miss CC about the supernatural, because she didn't know if she could be trusted! The girls were always taught to keep the identity of them being Anointeds a secret, otherwise it could put them in danger!

They were lucky that Rainn was just an Undutched! Suppose he was a Hazil, a Java or something worse! The girls knew they couldn't make that mistake again. All she could think about was Grandma V's warning.

Oliver climbed on Zoey's shoulder.

"Well, Zoey, Oliver has been with me for a very long time and now I'm giving him to you! He's fast and smart, he can get into places that you can't, and he may know a thing or two about," Miss CC leaned in once more, "the *supernatural*, not that it really exists—right?" She winked and smiled.

Zoey and Skylar laughed nervously.

Everyone had been paying so much attention to Oliver that they didn't realize that Abby was dressed!

"Well, I'm all set and ready to go!" Abby hollered as she spun around for everyone to see her poodle bathing suit, equipped with a tail and all!

"Why don't we go downstairs while the twins get ready? I can tell you how to take care of Oliver and you can show Zoey!" Miss CC said as she held Abby's hand. Abby leaped with joy as they headed downstairs.

"Supernatural, huh?" Miss CC mumbled.

Skylar reached in her closet and grabbed her bathing suit.

"Cover your eyes, Oliver. After all you are a boy!" Skylar ordered.

Oliver turned and faced the wall.

"Miss CC has got to know about the supernatural. How else can she have a rabbit that talks?" Skylar whispered while looking over her shoulder towards Oliver.

"How am I supposed to know?" Zoey lowered her voice to match Skylar's tone. Zoey didn't really care; she was just happy to have Oliver.

"Do you think she's an Anointed?" Skylar's eyes were wide.

"Maybe," Zoey nonchalantly replied.

Oliver sat listening to the girls intently.

CHAPTER 13

RAINN RETURNS!

Skylar and Zoey came downstairs in their one-piece matching orange bathing suits. They had always been fond of the color orange! Zoey held Oliver in her arms as if she were cradling a baby.

Oliver didn't like it very much, but he held his peace! After all, he just met the twins and wasn't willing to make any waves—not yet at least!

"Okay, we can go now." Skylar grabbed Abby's hand.

"Oh, girls, you go on ahead! I'll catch up!" Miss CC held the house keys in her hand.

The girls shrugged their shoulders and proceeded to walk out the door.

Cassey, why would you offer to take them to the pool when you know you have nothing but heels and dress clothes on? she thought to herself.

She noticed that when she placed her umbrella in the closet, it was a *shoe closet.* "Maybe their mom is a size eight in shoes," she said while searching for any pair of comfortable shoes she could find. Luckily, there were sandals in the closet. She slipped her feet inside.

"Darn it!" she moaned. The shoes were a size nine! They were awfully big. Still, it was better than wearing her heels to the pool! Miss CC headed out the door. She paused for a moment while gazing down at her dress. Borrowing shoes was one thing, but it would be hard to explain going through Mrs. Sway's bedroom closet. "Oh well, I guess I'm going to be really overdressed for the pool!" she replied as she locked the door.

It was a hot sunny day. Ms. Parker's dog was barking at them and pulling on his chain as usual.

"Boy is it hot out here!" Skylar wiped the sweat dripping down her face.

"My hair is soaked, and I haven't even gotten in the pool yet!"

"I'll say! My hair is dripping with sweat, too!" Zoey replied.

Rainn was hiding behind a fence. He leaped out in front of the girls.

"Well, hello girls! My name is Rainn, ask me again and I'll tell you the same!" Rainn danced in a circle around them with a large smile.

Abby found Rainn's silly dance quite amusing, "Hi Rainn!" she giggled.

Surprisingly enough, Abby was happy to see Rainn.

Oliver crawled on Skylar's back and remained hidden; he thought Rainn looked suspicious.

"So Rainn, tell me, why did you lie about being a Miran?!" Zoey demanded an explanation.

"Well, I didn't really lie, just give me some time, and I'll tell you why!" Rainn pulled a two-foot clock out of his coat pocket.

Again, Abby giggled.

Skylar and Zoey wondered how on earth Rainn could fit that large clock inside his pocket.

"Aren't you hot, Rainn?" Skylar couldn't help but notice Rainn was wearing a rather large coat.

"Why didn't you just say that you needed some shade? Just give me the test and I'll make the grade!" Rainn pulled out a huge multicolored umbrella!

"This is so embarrassing, put that umbrella away!" Zoey looked around to ensure no one was watching.

Skylar leaned over and whispered into Rainn's ear. "Don't mind her, she's just a little moody today."

Although the umbrella's appearance wasn't flattering, Zoey couldn't help but admit that it did keep the sun out of their faces.

"Well, I love the umbrella!" Abby snatched the umbrella out of Rainn's hand.

"No!!" he shouted. Rainn knew that the umbrella weighed more than Abby.

Abby wasn't heavy enough to hold it down, so the umbrella began to lift her up off the ground. Just then a northern wind blew and within moments, Abby was floating up, up, up the street!

"What did you do?!" Zoey yelled as she chased after Abby.

Skylar stood still, impatiently tapping her right foot against the sidewalk. "Well Rainn, say some of your fancy rhymes and bring her back!"

"You don't understand, I can't! I can only do a few tricks! I travel with the umbrella just for kicks!" he screeched as he chased after Abby and Zoey.

Oliver's ears were flopping in the wind. "Now what? I knew he seemed strange."

"You know Oliver, I'm beginning to share your opinion," Zoey surmised while gasping for air.

Skylar pressed her hands together and began to silently ask *God* for help! Suddenly the northern wind began to alter its course, and it blew in a southern direction! Abby started to slowly glide back to where she was carried from. She breezed past Zoey, Oliver, and Rainn and landed in Skylar's arms.

"Wow! That was so much fun!" Abby yelled.

To their surprise, while they were terrified, Abby was enjoying the ride!

Zoey and Rainn returned to Skylar, both out of breath and soaking in sweat.

"You could have saved me a trip if you told me that you were going to intervene," Zoey gasped.

"I didn't intervene Zoey, *God* did!"

"Can I do it again, Rainn?" Abby asked with hope in her eyes.

Skylar whispered in Zoey's ear. "Since when did she become Rainn's biggest fan?" she snickered.

"I was thinking the exact same thing!"

Zoey marched over to Abby and took the umbrella out of her hands and forced it into Rainn's.

"Here!"

Skylar was staring at Rainn. "Wait a minute, how did you know how and where to find us?"

"Yeah! How did you know?" Zoey wondered with inquisitive eyes.

Rainn began to kick his feet on the pavement as if he had reverted back to being a child! "Well, I sort of followed you... BUT it was only to make sure you got home safely!"

Zoey's cheeks were flushed, "YOU FOLLOWED US!" her eyes widened. And she repeated it again. "I can't believe you followed us!"

It was true, he followed them the day before from Grandma Victdamol's house as well, but he didn't want them to know how he found them on their walk today.

"Rainn, maybe you should go," Skylar insisted as she headed in the direction of the pool.

Everyone followed closely behind …everyone except Abby, that was!

"Guys," Abby whined.

The twins continued with their conversation; they didn't hear Abby at all.

"Rainn, Grandma V doesn't like you around us," Zoey interjected.

"I know she doesn't girls, but I want to help you. In order to gain favor and fully become an Anointed I must prove that I'm good! So, I thought to myself, what better way to become an Anointed than by helping one?! So here I am. I'm here to HELP!" Rainn responded with a warm smile.

"Help? Help with what?" Skylar inquired impatiently.

"Whatever it is that you're preparing for! Aren't you girls preparing for something big?" He leaned in closer in hopes that the girls would reveal some deep secret.

"Guys! What's going on?!" Abby yelled.

Skylar and Zoey turned around and Abby was about twenty feet behind them!

"What are you doing back there Abby?" Zoey asked as she motioned for Abby to run towards them.

"I can't move! I'm stuck!" Abby squealed.

Rainn, Skylar, and Zoey ran back towards Abby.

The girls and Rainn couldn't see in the *spiritual realm,* but there were two small demons holding Abby's feet!

Oliver, however, could *see* them and he whispered in Zoey's ears. "There are two demons holding her. Speak to them with authority and they will flee!"

Zoey's eyes darted. "Two demons?" she mumbled to herself. She wondered if what Oliver was saying could possibly be true!

The girls pulled on one side of Abby and Rainn pulled on the other. But Abby's body just swung from side to side, and she nearly knocked the twins over!

"Try lifting her," Skylar suggested.

Rainn went over to Abby. He pulled and pulled, but nothing happened! Abby was not budging!

Off in the distance, Miss CC was walking up the pavement. Her feet were awkwardly sliding back and forth in their mom's shoes. She would stop momentarily, adjusting her feet in the sandals. Nevertheless, this didn't appear to slow her down much!

"What do we do?" the girls asked Rainn.

"Your gift is greater than mine! I don't know, but you're running out of time!" Rainn scurried out of sight.

CHAPTER 14

WHO INVITED THEM?

"You coward!" Zoey shouted.

Skylar turned around. "Miss CC is getting closer. She's almost here! How on earth can we explain this?"

Zoey turned towards Oliver, who gave her a smile of encouragement, "trust me!" he whispered, "speak with authority!"

Zoey turned to her sisters. "I think I know what's going on."

Ollie gave Zoey a gentle smile and a wink of encouragement.

Zoey figured what they were doing wasn't working, so why not try what Oliver suggested?

"Demons flee, in the name of *Jesus Christ!*" she demanded.

Suddenly, the demons heard the authority in her voice, and they disappeared!

Zoey wondered how Oliver could see in the *spiritual realm*. She once again recalled the story of Balaam and his donkey. In the *Bible* the donkey had the ability to *speak* and see in the *spiritual realm*. However, Balaam couldn't see in the *spiritual realm*. The donkey was able to communicate with his owner Balaam. The donkey was trying to protect him.

When Zoey looked up, Miss CC was standing directly behind Abby!

"Nice of you girls to wait for me." She placed her hand on Abby's shoulder and paused to gain a moment of rest. Her feet were hurting so bad that she would rather sit down on the hot pavement than walk another two feet without a break.

The girls didn't want to respond, because they knew that it wasn't true. There was an awkward silence. Abby remained still.

Miss CC wondered what was going on, but she decided not to ask.

Miss CC looked down at Abby, "Well...let's go!"

Abby raised her eyebrows and turned to Skylar and Zoey, but she remained perfectly still. She was waiting for her big sisters to confirm that the issue was resolved, and she could move.

Miss CC paused and gazed at the girls with her hands positioned on her hips, "Okay girls—is there a problem?" She had a slight chuckle in her tone.

Abby turned to Skylar. "I don't know … Is there a problem, Skylar?"

Skylar looked at Zoey. "I don't know …Is there a problem, Zoey?"

Zoey questioned Oliver. "Is there a problem Ollie?"

Oliver gave Zoey a confident smile. "Not that I can *see!*"

"No problem at all Miss CC! Abby just had a little something stuck on her sandals." Zoey gave Abby a wink.

Abby took a step forward. "Wow! You're the best, Zoey!"

Miss CC had a confused look on her face but continued to walk. Oliver snuck from behind Zoey. "Boy, that was close," he whispered.

Once the girls got to the neighborhood pool, they saw a few kids from their school. *Some* they were happy to see, others not so much!

"Okay kids, I know the drill. You don't want anyone to know that you have a babysitter." Miss CC scanned the pool area. "I'm going to go over to the soda machine and take Oliver with me." She opened her bag, and he hopped in.

As Miss CC was walking away, Zoey mumbled, "she kind of grows on you."

Both Abby and Skylar nodded in agreement.

Mathew Corker was on the diving board. He was the last person Zoey wanted to see! He lived in their neighborhood, went to their school, AND rode their bus! Zoey was looking forward to not seeing Mathew at all this summer. She was disappointed her wish didn't come true. She supposed Mathew was nice, but he was the kind of kid who was always following people around and asking five hundred questions.

"Hi Zoey!" he hollered as he dived in the water.

She threw a half wave at Mathew. She sped up the pace in hopes of discouraging him from trying to catch up to them.

Skylar laughed as she observed her sister.

"Well, besides Stephanie, he's the only other kid at school that can actually tell us apart," Skylar noted.

"Unfortunately," Zoey moaned to herself. "Besides, I don't understand why it's so confusing to everyone else. I'm obviously the prettier one!"

Skylar rolled her eyes. They continued to walk Abby over to the kiddie pool. Her sister was talking nonsense and she wasn't going to entertain it! As she turned around, she bumped into none other than Jake!

Jake didn't live in the neighborhood, but he often took the trail through the woods which connected their communities. He often managed to sneak his way into their neighborhood pool.

"Well, if it isn't the three ugly sisters!" he insulted while wiping snot from his nose.

Skylar frowned. "Gross."

The snot ran down Jake's hands and he managed to ignore it, which the twins weren't the least bit surprised about.

Abby balled her fists. "I've had about enough of you!"

"Don't sweat it, kid. I've got bigger fish to fry than the three of you!" His eyebrows lifted as he spotted a more interesting *target.*

Jake was staring at a kid on the opposite end of the pool. "Hey Pauly, where's my soda money?!" He yelled.

"Lucky for us. Maybe he'll leave us alone this summer," Zoey suggested.

Skylar pointed with a frown. "Yeah, as long as Pauly is around." she said disapprovingly.

The girls could see Stephanie's ponytail swinging from side to side as she came bouncing towards them. The new neighbor and some other girls were trailing her.

Zoey wondered why Stephanie was with them. Stephanie had also failed to mention the fact that she was coming to the pool. Although, Zoey conveniently didn't seem to recall the fact that they failed to invite Stephanie to the pool as well.

"Hey girls!" Stephanie yelled as she managed to dodge splashing water that was coming from the pool.

"Hi Stephanie. Summer just started and you're looking to replace us already," Zoey said in a sarcastic tone, as she scanned past Stephanie and stared at the other girls.

Stephanie caught the sarcasm in Zoey's tone. But she knew Zoey long enough to determine that there was some truth in her sarcasm! She figured she had better *fix it* and fast! After all, she didn't want her best friends to be upset with her.

She nervously cleared her throat, "I figured I'd show them around... ya know? Be a good neighbor." She paused and waited anxiously for the twins' responses.

"*Sure.*" Skylar replied. She didn't have an issue with Stephanie being friends with anyone.

Zoey was silent for the span of a couple of seconds. Skylar nudged Zoey's shoulder. "Of course, Stephanie, we understand," Zoey replied.

Zoey's attention turned from Stephanie and the other girls to Ollie.

She knew that Oliver was safe with Miss CC, but she was still missing her new friend.

Stephanie noticed that Zoey appeared a little distracted and Skylar was unusually quiet. Stephanie figured the best thing to do was lighten the mood! She cleared her throat once more. "Well, girls, let me introduce you to Alexia's sisters: Chloe, Tammy, and Rhonda."

Skylar and Zoey didn't previously realize that the other girls with Alexia and Stephanie were her sisters.

"Well, it's nice to meet all of you and welcome to Oldsville Terrace," Skylar added. "We introduced ourselves to Alexia the other day! But I'm Skylar and this is my sister Zoey!" She pulled Zoey towards the girls. "And that's our sister Abby, splashing over there in the kiddie pool."

The new neighbors waved.

"Tammy, why don't you go and play with Abby in the pool," Alexia insisted as she winked at her sister.

"Oh sure, right…I'll play with her," Tammy replied as she did a cannon ball into the pool and the water went all over Rhonda.

"So uncool!" Rhonda said as she excused herself to get a towel to dry off.

Alexia and Chloe plastered a fake smile on their faces.

The girls stood in awkward silence. The silence was deafening to Skylar, she just couldn't take it anymore.

She searched her mind for something they could talk about. "Well, how do you all like Oldsville Terrace so far?"

"It seems pretty cool. What do you guys do for fun around here? Besides going to the pool?" Alexia had an inquisitive look on her face.

Skylar and Zoey noticed that Tammy was the only one dressed in a bathing suit. They quickly assumed that the pool wasn't really the girls' *thing*.

"Well, sometimes we go to Parkers Mall and play in the arcade room," replied Skylar.

"Arcade room? What's that?" Chloe had a smug look on her face.

Finally, they were talking about something that was worthy of Zoey's attention! Zoey's focus turned immediately from Miss CC and Oliver, and she inserted herself into the conversation.

"Did you say, what's that...? Did you really say what's that?!" Zoey repeated with her mouth wide open.

Zoey wasn't into the PlayStation, Nintendo, or the Xbox. But sit her in an *old-school* arcade, and you'd have to serve her breakfast, lunch, and dinner right there!

Zoey continued. "An arcade is a place where there are video games everywhere. Not just *any* video games—no I mean the best! We're talkin' Pac-Man, Donkey Kong, Mario Bros., Centipede...the *originals*! The games that started it all!"

It was clear that Zoey's body was at the pool, but her mind was at the arcade! She could barely contain her excitement.

"Okay!" Alexia snickered while rolling her eyes. "Maybe you can take us there and we can hang out a bit." Alexia knew this was an opportunity to get to know the twins, draw them in— get them to trust them. *We have to build a rapport with them.* Alexia thought while trying not to gag.

"Of course! We'll be glad to," Zoey shrieked with a burst of excitement in her voice.

Chloe stood there with her arms folded. Unmoved and even less amused with the whole situation. "Sounds like a stupid place," she mumbled.

Alexia nudged her sister's shoulder in hopes that she would remember *why* they were trying to build a relationship with the girls.

"I mean, it sounds good!" Chloe agreed in a non-convincing tone.

It was too late for Chloe to fix it! Zoey had already heard the comment Chloe made. She didn't like it one bit! And she was beginning to dislike her. Zoey didn't appreciate the insult about the game room! She took the remark personally!

"Hey guys, I bet I can beat all of you in a race across the pool!" Alexia said, in an attempt to take everyone's attention off her sister Chloe. Alexia removed her shorts and t-shirt, and it immediately revealed a hidden bathing suit.

Guess they like the pool after all, the twins thought.

Alexia's idea worked.

"You're on!" the girls screamed as they dived into the water.

CHAPTER 15

THE CAT'S MEOW!

Hours had gone by, and the girls were on their way home. Miss CC remained a safe distance behind the girls in order to keep from embarrassing them! She remembered what it was like to be a kid and not wanting to be teased for having a babysitter.

"So, how long have you guys lived here?" Alexia asked.

"All of our lives. We really like it." Skylar glanced back at Miss CC to ensure that she was a safe distance behind them.

As the girls were talking, Zoey felt uncomfortable. She couldn't quite put her finger on it, but she believed there was something strange about the neighbors.

"Why is your sister so quiet?" Alexia's eyes shifted back and forth from one twin to the other.

"Oh, that's just Zoey; she goes through mood swings from time to time."

Alexia pushed her hair out of her face and rolled her eyes. *We've got to make friends with them,* she reminded herself once more. She continued. "Well, I have three sisters, so I know what it's like when one is moody." Alexia shot a comforting smile in Skylar's direction.

Zoey had overheard Skylar and Alexia's conversation.

"I'm not moody. I've just got more important things on my mind." Zoey wrinkled her forehead.

Chloe glared at Zoey; She was looking for any reason to get into a fight with her. Heck, she used any reason to get into a confrontation with *anyone!* Zoey stared back at Chloe with just as much irritation in her eyes. Zoey wasn't afraid of her; in fact, she was just as tough!

Stephanie couldn't help but notice the tension. She was well aware that Zoey wouldn't back down. She got between them and put her arms around both Chloe and Zoey.

Alexia knew that if Chloe and Zoey argued, it would put their mission in jeopardy.

Alexia motioned for Rhonda, Tammy, and Chloe to walk ahead.

"Well, it was nice hanging with y'all, but this is our stop." Skylar pointed to their house.

Rhonda stood marveling at the brick steps that led to a beautiful brick home with red shutters. Rhonda noticed that their home appeared a lot newer than the other homes in the neighborhood. She admired how well Skylar and Zoey's parents had kept up the place.

Abby pulled Tammy's arm. She wanted to show Tammy her dog, Shye.

"Oh, so this is where y'all live. Nice house! Maybe we can come over tomorrow and hang out," Alexia replied.

Zoey did not respond; she was hoping that Skylar wouldn't either.

Suddenly, Shye started to dodge around Abby and head towards the neighbors. He continued to bark over and over. Skylar and Zoey were surprised because Shye was friendly to everyone!

Skylar picked Shye up. She was embarrassed by his behavior. "I don't know what's gotten into him!" Skylar's attention turned back to Alexia. "Of course, you can come by tomorrow!"

Alexia knew that their dog Shye had *sensed* that her and her sisters were evil. Quite often, many animals and babies were able to *discern* them. She could tell that Zoey was becoming suspicious by Shye's response towards them. She knew exactly how to distract Zoey.

"Hey Zoey, when we come over tomorrow, why don't you take us to the arcade room you've been talking about?"

Zoey's attention quickly shifted, "Sure! It's close enough that we can walk! We can meet here tomorrow at about 3:00."

Skylar did a half smile; she knew that Zoey was only onboard because they agreed to do something *she* liked!

"Cool, we'll see you then. "Alexia smiled with satisfaction that she had distracted Zoey once again!

The neighbors and Stephanie walked down the road talking to one another. Skylar couldn't help but notice that their sister Rhonda kept gazing back at them. She was smiling but at the same time, she appeared sad.

"Come on Skylar!" Zoey called.

****

The girls had always enjoyed spending time with their parents. It consisted of lots of board games, movies, and popcorn! They had just finished beating their parents at Connect Four and ate so much pizza that they would burst if they got another slice. Things were beginning to wind down and the girls were now in their room putting on their nightgowns.

Skylar was rolling her hair as she glanced in the mirror and saw her sister's reflection. It was the perfect time for her to get answers to some questions she pondered about all day. Zoey was sitting on the bed scratching Oliver's back.

"Higher...just a little higher," Ollie whined.

"Zoey, what do you think about Alexia?" Skylar's mouth was twisted to the side.

Zoey ignored Skylar's question. "I'm excited about taking them to the arcade." Her eyes lit up once again. And then her smile diminished. "But it's just *something* about them."

Skylar was eager to make new friends! Stephanie was the girls' only *real* friend in their neighborhood. Zoey on the other hand was always a loner. She didn't mind it just being the two of them, and Steph, of course!

Skylar jumped on her bed. "Well, they all seem cool to me, especially Alexia." Skylar placed her finger on her chin. "Well except for Chloe. She seems a little grouchy."

"I'll say!" Zoey stopped scratching Ollie.

Skylar studied her sister for a moment, "I think she hurt your feelings. That's why you don't like her very much." Skylar rested her hands on her chin and she continued. "You just watch, the two of you will be the best of friends before summer is out!"

Zoey squinted. She barely spoke to Chloe. She couldn't imagine why her sister would say such a thing.

Zoey had a bizarre look on her face. "Why would I want to be best friends with Chloe?"

"I figure you grouches like to stick together!" Skylar laughed as she rolled back and forth on her bed.

"*Ha! Ha!*" Zoey tossed a pillow in her direction." Zoey's face was now serious. "I just don't trust her, or her sisters for that matter! I can't explain it, it just doesn't *feel* right." Zoey glanced over at Shye who found a ball lying in the corner and decided to chase it around the room! She stood up and pointed at him. "Even Shye doesn't like them!"

Skylar knew that Zoey had a point about Shye. He liked everyone! He even greeted the mailman when he came!

Nevertheless, Skylar was looking forward to a fun summer and having new friends to add into the mix could only make it that much more exciting!

"Here you go again Zoey! Always judging people without taking the time to get to know them!"

Zoey gazed in the mirror and began brushing her hair. "You think you know it all, but you know nothing. I'm telling you; something isn't right about them!"

Oliver didn't want the girls to argue. He decided he had better be the mediator in the situation. Although he had been there a short time, he wasn't used to seeing them act like this.

"Girls please stop!! Do you think either of you know them enough to decide if you like them or not?" Oliver was standing on Zoey's bed. Zoey and Skylar both shrugged their shoulders.

"Well then, you're sisters. You shouldn't be arguing with each other," he continued as he wiggled his way to the foot of the bed.

Zoey and Skylar felt silly for allowing perfect strangers to cause them to be at odds with one another!

"Hey, who cares about the new neighbors anyway?" Skylar winked at her sister.

"I guess you do. You're the one that's talking about it," Zoey remarked.

"You're right! Maybe the argument I should have been making is why I shouldn't have been a twin," Skylar joked.

"Oh no, I would definitely win that argument!" Zoey giggled.

They began to toss their pillows back and forth once more and laughed uncontrollably. Their door flung open, and Abby breezed in with her dolls in her arms. "You guys are always having fun without me!" she squealed with pouted lips.

"You know you're always welcome in our room, squirt." Zoey affectionately pinched Abby's nose.

Screech! Screech!

Suddenly, there was a sound that echoed throughout the room! The twins turned to one another to see if perhaps the other was making the noise. Abby was bouncing a basketball back and forth against the wall. The girls paused quietly to try and differentiate the sounds. It was clear that *this* sound was not coming from the ball.

"Shh." Zoey motioned for Abby to stop bouncing the ball.

Abby disappointingly did a swift kick, and the ball rolled under the bunkbed.

"What is that?" Skylar whispered as she trudged towards the sound.

It was like a scene out of an old horror movie! Every instinct the girls had, told them to run away, hide, and scream for their mom and dad! But curiosity got the best of them! They listened closely to investigate which direction the sound was coming from. They instantaneously determined that it was coming from the window! Skylar and Zoey inched closer and closer to the window, while ducking down in the process, in order to remain hidden from the culprit. The sound was a screeching noise as if something was scratching against the window.

"I wouldn't do that if I were you," Oliver cautioned as he covered a part of his ear with one paw.

The twins dismissed Oliver's warning and continued with their mission. Skylar and Zoey's window was opened halfway, so it allowed a cool breeze to flow throughout the room. Skylar was kicking herself, wishing she had listened to Zoey earlier when she told her to close the window. She now hoped that whatever was on the other side of the window wasn't small enough to get in through the opening.

Abby whispered, "I don't know if this is such a good idea!" as she cowered behind the bed.

They glanced back at their little sister, making sure she was a safe distance away, then they continued towards the window. The closer they got; they noticed a white liquid slowly trickling down the windowsill.

Skylar rubbed the wet substance between her fingers and held it to her nose.

"What is it?" Zoey inquired.

Skylar stood with a perplexed look on her face, "It's...MILK."

"MILK?" Zoey grabbed her sister's hand and smelled her fingertips for herself.

She shot a look of confusion in her sister's direction.

Skylar lifted the window up and suddenly there appeared a *cat* floating in midair! The cat had one paw with very sharp claws scratching against the twins' window!

It was significantly larger than a house cat—at least three times the size! It had hair that was reminiscent of a lion's mane around its face, and its hair stood up like the petals of a sunflower on a hot summer's day—swaying back and forth in the direction the wind blew.

The cat's eyes were dark, and laser focused on Skylar and Zoey. It was brown with black spots all around it. Its mouth was rather large and unusually wide for a cat! It was plump as if it was accustomed to eating multiple meals a day. The cat's tail was short, and it had long curly whiskers.

The girls screamed. "What is that?!"

The flying cat stared at them. Its mouth turned into a snarl. "What do I look like? I'm a CAT!" it replied with frustration in its voice. "You are indeed from the bloodline of the Hartfords, and you will be the demise of your family! For many years there have been those that have wanted to destroy your family, but they were weaker and could not succeed. Now you've finally met your match!" the cat hissed.

Skylar's fear diminished and it was replaced by anger. She placed one fist up in the air. "Stay away from my family!"

Zoey was typically the one that was always ready for a fight, but a flying cat was a little out of her league! The cat's words had pierced Zoey like a sword! She took refuge behind her sister.

The cat opened its mouth, and its sharp teeth began to show! It opened its mouth even wider, hissed, and a horrible odor came out! The odor smelled like a combination of week-old fish mixed with a skunk and rotten eggs! The aroma was so strong that the girls immediately distanced themselves even further from the cat. They took their hands and covered their noses!

"You haven't seen the last of me!" the cat warned as it flew away.

Oliver was crouched on the side of the bed hiding next to Abby.

Skylar closed the window and locked it tight! She was once again kicking herself for not locking it earlier!

Skylar ran towards the fan and turned it on.

Zoey bolted towards the door. "We've got to tell Mom and Dad," she said in between coughs.

Skylar grabbed Zoey's arm and pulled her back. "Tell them what? That a flying cat that smells like a skunk, flew up two floors and threatened our family?!" Skylar declared passionately with a puzzled look on her face. She knew that their parents wouldn't believe a word they said. *Who would?*

Zoey pulled her arm back. "Well, that's what happened, isn't it?!" She faced Abby and Oliver. She was in search of backup!

Oliver stood whistling in the corner and looking around the room as if he was oblivious to what had just happened.

Zoey's gaze moved to Abby.

Abby looked around. "Who me?"

Zoey folded her arms and stared at Abby.

Abby became uncomfortable, "Hey, don't ask me. I'm just a little kid," She grabbed her dolls, and eased towards the door.

Zoey looked at both Oliver and Abby; she felt abandoned.

Skylar plopped on her bed. "They will think we're crazy! Why don't we call Grandma V tomorrow? She'll listen to us!"

Skylar reassured herself that she was making the right decision. "Yeah, she'll know what to do!"

Zoey sat there with her arms folded. She refused to side with her sister, and she definitely wasn't making any eye contact!

Skylar let out a big sigh. "Well, what do you think Ollie?"

Ollie was more concerned with his behavior. He couldn't believe he ran and hid with Abby when he was supposed to be *protecting* the girls! He felt like he lived up to the name—*scaredy* cat! He promptly dismissed his thoughts, attempting to reassure himself that the girls didn't observe his coward-like behavior! With his hand clenched behind his back, he paced back and forth at an attempt to look intellectual.

"Well…Skylar, you may be right. Your parents probably won't believe you. But if you think your grandma *will*, then just talk to *her*. The important thing is you all are reaching out to an adult that you trust!" He twitched his nose from side to side. "It's obvious someone must have sent it, and they want to destroy your whole family. Who could want you gone and why?"

Skylar and Zoey didn't know who could be behind the mysterious visit from *the flying cat!* They didn't even know that flying cats *existed!* "I don't know. I mean, we don't have any enemies or anything," Zoey noted.

"Zoey, we're Anointeds. Grandma V says that Anointeds *always* have enemies, remember? Anything that's not part of the *LIGHT* is a potential enemy!" Skylar paced around the room. "We've learned about Javas, Hazels, and the Undutched, but Grandma V forgot to *tell* us about *talking animals!*" Skylar noted as her eyes darted in Oliver's direction.

It didn't matter how subtle Skylar was trying to be, Oliver noticed. "I prefer to be called a gentleman rather than an animal—thank you!" he replied in a stern tone.

Skylar felt bad for offending Ollie.

Abby finally spoke up. "I don't know, that was pretty scary. Maybe we *should* call Grandma V." She snapped her fingers. "Or… maybe it was one of Grandma V's tests."

But the twins knew that Grandma V would never test them at home.

Abby huddled between her two sisters. "I'm really scared."

"Don't be afraid, Abby. We're going to get to the bottom of this!" Skylar replied.

CHAPTER 16

A LIGHT TO GUIDE THE WAY!

Then spake Jesus again unto them, saying, I am the light of the world: he that followeth me shall not walk in darkness, but shall have the light of life.

(John 8:12)

The girls were up bright and early! Miss CC had officially been hired to babysit Skylar, Zoey, and Abby off and on for the summer. Their mom had decided to let Nick remain in daycare so the girls could be free to go to the park, pool, and do other activities. They had quickly grown quite fond of Miss CC. After all, she did bring Oliver into their lives!

However, they still preferred spending the summer with Grandma V. What happened the night before gave them the perfect excuse to call their grandma. The twins tried to call her multiple times, but they were unsuccessful. They grew anxious by the moment and needed to find out who this mysterious cat was.

"Well, Grandma V isn't answering!" Skylar sat wondering who else would be wise enough to assist them with this matter. She snapped her fingers and swung her head towards her sister. "Maybe Ms. Bell can help!"

Ms. Bell was also an Anointed and happened to be a very good friend of Grandma V.

Zoey was unamused by the suggestion; she knew the only way to discuss anything with Ms. Bell was to go visit her. After all, the girls didn't have her phone number. But Zoey had to admit that Ms. Bell probably could help them! Besides, Ms. Bell lived much closer than Grandma V so the girls could walk there.

"And what do you suppose we tell Miss CC?" Zoey's forehead wrinkled.

Skylar leaned forward, "why don't we tell her that we're going to see a friend?"

"Well, that could work. Ms. Bell is a friend of the family, so it is the truth. It wouldn't take too long to get there and get back," Zoey replied.

Oliver snuck out of the room to visit Miss CC. She was sitting at the table sipping her coffee. She had just finished making breakfast and was excited to see Oliver. Miss CC leaped from her seat and squeezed Ollie.

"Even though it's only been a day, I didn't realize I was going to miss you so much!"

Oliver hopped on the stool next to Miss CC. His face was serious, and Miss CC quickly realized that this wasn't a social call.

"The girls must go on a mission. They're going to see someone named Ms. Bell, but they're going to tell you that they are going to just see a friend. Don't insist on coming and please don't question them. This is very important!" he emphasized while munching on a carrot.

Miss CC was concerned about Skylar and Zoey, but she knew whatever they were up to must be very important!

"Very well, I won't give them a hard time...on one condition." She leaned in closer to Oliver.

"Sure, *anything*," Ollie smiled.

"You have to go with them and keep them safe!" Miss CC leaned back with her arms folded and eyebrows raised. She knew that Oliver wasn't very brave, but she had confidence that deep down inside he would grow to rely on his instincts and help the twins.

Oliver, on the other hand, sat there bewildered. He thought that Miss CC's trust and faith in him was misguided. He didn't believe he was who she aspired him to be, but he didn't have the heart, nor the desire to tarnish the image she had of him.

"Of course, I will," he said as his eyes nervously eyeballed the floor.

As if the girls knew Ollie and Miss CC were done talking, they came into the kitchen right on cue and grabbed a piece of their respective fruits.

"Miss CC, can we run to a friend's house? It's not far and we'll be back before lunch." Zoey began to babble.

Miss CC ignored the question and couldn't help but notice that the girls didn't bother to eat the breakfast she made. "You girls aren't going to eat any of the breakfast I prepared?" she asked disappointingly.

Ollie gave Miss CC a stern look. She quickly remembered that she wasn't supposed to give the girls a hard time! She cleared her throat. "Of course, girls. Don't take too long. A piece of fruit will suit you just fine."

"Don't worry, Miss CC. I'm not going. I'll eat the breakfast," Abby squealed.

Miss CC was embarrassed, and she gave a sobering look in Ollie's direction.

"Okay, Abby!" Miss CC gave a gentle smile as she slid a plate of food in Abby's direction.

Skylar, Zoey, and Ollie left out the front door.

"That was a lot easier than I thought it would be," Zoey admitted.

Oliver stood smiling, feeling proud of himself.

****

The girls left the house and hiked into the woods behind their neighborhood. Alexia and her sisters were not far behind. The neighbors' mother had the flying cat keeping tabs on the girls! When it overheard that the twins would be leaving their home, she reported back to Lucinda McClaire, who then ordered the neighbors to follow them.

"Where are they going?" Alexia whispered. Her voice slightly echoed through the woods.

Zoey stopped in her tracks and positioned her hand in front of her sister. Ollie and Skylar came to a screeching halt!

"Did you hear that?" Zoey whispered as she paused and glanced around her. There were large trees casting a shadow upon the ground and various spurts of wind cascading the leaves in never ending circles. The only sound was a gentle whistle as if the leaves were engaged in their own conversation!

Zoey knew she heard *something or even...someone,* but Skylar dismissed it as paranoia and continued her quest.

"I'm telling you I heard someone!" Zoey pleaded.

Skylar ignored her sister as she tried her best to avoid any spiders and other insects that crept and crawled in the woods.

The girls made their way up a hill. They were both trying to remember where Ms. Bell's house was, but for some reason, they just couldn't recall. It was as if something or *someone* had *blocked* their memory! They debated about whether they should turn around. The twins hesitated and with a mutual glance, they agreed to turn around without the exchange of one word!

They were headed back when a *light* appeared in the sky!

The light's glory had nothing to do with the sun. The light was white, radiant, and pulsated back and forth as if it were taking deep breaths—in and out! With each inhale, it grew dimmer. The exhales illuminated the light, and it *shined* even brighter than its previous pulsating!

This light appeared to be moving slowly, but it had a definite direction in mind! It glided and bounced from side to side as if it were a ping pong ball, swaying in and out of the trees' leaves. The twins immediately followed the *glorious* light and began to run through the woods.

The neighbors followed closely behind the twins. They saw Skylar and Zoey looking up in the sky, yet they were unable to *see the light.* The neighbors were full of darkness, and they were unable to lay eyes on the *light!* The twins weaved in and out of the bushes and jumped over logs. They did their best to keep up with the radiant light! They could now see off in the distance that the light suddenly came to a screeching halt! As they got past the trees, they could now see in the clearing that the light was sitting directly above—none other than Ms. Bell's home! The light had led the way!

They approached the familiar lake that rested in front of Ms. Bell's house.

Anytime Grandma V would take them to visit Ms. Bell, she would often have to wait near the lake and Ms. Bell would come out to meet her! Skylar and Zoey decided to do the same. They stared at the house and waited patiently.

The neighbors watched with curiosity. "What are they doing?" Chloe's tone revealed her aggravation. "This is such a waste of time!" she wined as she dug her heels in the ground.

"Shh!" Alexia stared at her sister with fire in her eyes!

Chloe decided to head back, and Tammy joined her. Chloe had a look of pride on her face as her little sister followed her away from the house. She enjoyed the fact that there was a *mini her,* sort of speak.

Rhonda looked at her sisters. Unlike Tammy, she didn't see anything worth admiring about her sister Chloe—nor Alexia for that matter! She was not amused by her sisters' behaviors. She loved her family, but she never felt like she fit in.

Her sisters were always plotting, being evil, and destructive. They couldn't be happy unless they were doing something to disrupt someone else's *life*! Rhonda on the other hand just wanted to be a kid! She always wondered what it would be like to be in a family that *loved* and didn't *hate*! Who brought joy instead of pain. Who was happy instead of spreading anger. Who didn't fear their mother but felt safe in her arms! A family like the ones she read about in her books!

Rhonda didn't understand what made her different from her family. She just knew that none of the evil brought her any pleasure! She wasn't sure how she could describe love because she had never been loved by her family. Or how to have peace when there had never been peace in her home. And joy and happiness were forbidden if it wasn't a celebration due to the result of someone else's destruction. All she knew was that the emotions, behaviors, and actions of her sisters didn't *feel* right to her!

In addition, those things didn't come natural to her like the others! She didn't envy Chloe like Tammy did. And her and Alexia were further opposites than the North and South Poles! Still, she believed that this must be her *destiny,* as Lucinda McClaire puts it!

"Rhonda!" Alexia's voice echoed in Rhonda's ear. "You're always daydreaming!" Alexia clapped her hands together. "Wake up!" she shouted.

Rhonda was used to being spoken to rudely by her sisters.

"Well, are you coming?" Alexia barked.

Rhonda hadn't realized that as she was lost in her thoughts, she had stopped walking. Rhonda didn't enjoy confrontation, unlike her other sister, Chloe.

Alexia had a way of asking a question yet demanding an action at the same time!

"Yes, of course Alexia." Rhonda resumed walking as the two of them followed the twins. However, they managed to keep a safe distance behind them.

A wind came from the east and then from the west. In the center of the lake there was a whirlwind which mirrored a miniature tornado! It spun around blending the colors red, orange, yellow, green, blue, indigo, and violet! It appeared as if a rainbow was imbedded in the midst of it.

The girls were astonished by the vibrant colors, and the flashes of light that seamlessly bounced off the reflection of the lake. The colors swirled for a moment and just as quickly as it rose from the waters, it collapsed and moved as waves across the lake. Skylar, Zoey, and Oliver were all mesmerized by the beauty of the water!

A petite, fully gray-haired woman with a round face and thick glasses resting slightly above the rim of her nose strolled out of the small house. She physically moved around like a rather young woman! She appeared to need no assistance from a cane even though she was almost 100 years old—like Grandma V. She had a smile that looked as if it was perfectly painted on her face! The corners of her mouth had a slight curve and rested with dimples on both sides.

In spite of her age, she had a spark of *youth* in her eyes! She didn't allow her age to interfere with her desire to help! Although she couldn't physically fight anymore, Ms. Bell still had a great deal of knowledge. It gave her great joy to assist young Anointeds on their journeys!

"My fellow Anointeds, please come near so that I can see you better," she called as she removed her glasses to wipe them. Ms.

Bell was *outlined* in light! They had seen this light before—around their own grandma!

There was only one problem, the lake was much wider than it was when they used to come visit with Grandma V. Ms. Bell could simply walk around the lake before! But not now!

"How do we cross?" they inquired of Ms. Bell.

"Just keep your eyes on *Jesus*! And don't get into *unbelief*!" Ms. Bell smiled. "With *Jesus* you can do the impossible," she responded with enthusiasm in her voice.

Suddenly, a shiny *Light* appeared beside Ms. Bell! This wasn't the same light that had led them to Ms. Bell's home. They automatically *knew* that *Jesus* was that *Light*! Just as Peter did in the *Bible*, the girls kept their eyes on *Jesus Christ* and began to *walk* across the water! They dared not take their eyes off the *Light* and walk in unbelief! They knew that once Peter's focus changed, and he started to be frightened, he began to sink. *Jesus* had to save him!

Slowly, they followed the *Light*, with Ollie clinging tightly to Zoey. Oliver wasn't sure that he understood what was going on. He took brief moments to look down and watch as the water rippled beneath the twins' feet. When their feet touched solid ground, just as quickly as the *Light* appeared—*He* was gone! The twins were elated! They had never walked on water before!

Alexia and Rhonda stood back observing. They had heard what the woman said, but because they were in darkness, they could not look upon the *Light* (*Jesus Christ*).

They were perplexed. Alexia and Rhonda didn't understand how Skylar and Zoey were able to walk on the water!

Surely it must be some sort of trick, Alexia thought. Her thoughts began to escape her. "Yeah, that's it! That old woman has some kind of platform beneath their feet!" she insisted.

Rhonda wrinkled her forehead and leaned a little closer while squinting her eyes. "I don't think so, Alexia. It looks like they just—" Rhonda hesitated for a moment, not knowing how her sister would react. She took a big gulp and continued, "walked on water!"

"No one can walk on water!" Alexia spat. "Don't you know that?"

Alexia knew her explanation was silly, but it was better than accepting the fact that the twins could do something supernatural, that her and her sisters...nor Lucinda McClaire herself could do! She would have to admit that the Anointeds source of *power* was greater than the Hazils. And she wasn't willing to do that!

Rhonda didn't want to argue with her sister; she knew there was no point! Alexia would only get enraged. And when Tammy and Chloe found out, they were sure to take her side—as usual! She pretended to agree with her sister, but she knew that what they just witnessed was some sort of miracle! She had seen her mother do many things.

However, walking on water wasn't one of them! Rhonda wondered to herself what made the twins different from her and her family. What or *WHO* gave them the ability to do such a thing? Whoever was behind this must hold great power!

Rhonda mustered the courage to respond. "Yeah, Alexia you're right. What was I thinking? It must be some platform of some sort." Rhonda's eyes quickly darted in a direction away from her sister in hopes that she couldn't tell she was lying.

Alexia stood with her arms folded and a cryptic smile upon her face, nodding her head in agreement.

CHAPTER 17

NARRATOR'S CORNER

So did you know that there are times God speaks to you in your dreams?! That's really exciting isn't it! *God* does this for many different reasons! First and foremost, *God* communicates with you because *He* loves you! Some dreams may reveal something pertaining to the future or perhaps your calling.

For example, in the book of Genesis, Pharoah had a dream warning him about a food shortage that would occur and last for seven years. *God* used Joseph to interpret the dream for Pharoah and because of *God's* grace and mercy, Pharoah was able to prepare ahead of the famine, and they still had plenty!

Daniel was given dreams by *God* about the future as well! Joseph, the husband of Mary had an angel visit him in a dream, and the angel told him it was okay to take Mary as his wife. He was also given a dream that told him to flee because *Jesus,* (as a baby) was in danger.

Do you remember when King Solomon had a dream and *God* appeared and asked him what he wanted to be given, and Solomon asked for wisdom?

There are countless others who have had dreams from *God* in the *Bible*, and that's one way *God* still communicates today! You should pay attention to your dreams, and any that may seem significant, write them in a journal. It may appear to mean nothing now, but one day you may realize that it was a message from *God Himself!*

Skylar's dream was also significant because it held the key to what the deception was. She just hadn't figured it out yet!

For God speaketh once, yea twice, yet man perceiveth it not. In a dream, in a vision of the night, when deep sleep falleth upon men, in slumberings upon the bed; then he openeth the ears of men and sealeth their instruction.

(Job 33:14-16)

CHAPTER 18

DISCERNMENT IS IMPORTANT!

"*Great is your FAITH! That's why you were able to walk across the water!* Come inside, I have much to share with you!" Ms. Bell did a slight hop to show her enthusiasm and led the way.

As Ms. Bell turned again to enter her home, there was a gust of wind that blew! The wind almost knocked Alexia and Rhonda off their feet. It was as if it was disciplining them for eavesdropping!

Skylar and Zoey had never been in Ms. Bell's home before. They had only come there with Grandma V and each time they spoke outside.

The twins entered the small house and glanced around the room. They couldn't help but notice there were *NO* televisions, or computers. Come to mention it, there wasn't much technology at all! Zoey couldn't imagine how she could *survive* without her video games and movies! There was an old burgundy chair that sat in the corner and a little round table with four chairs that rested in the middle of the room. There were three plates with brownies on them. Two plates had a glass of milk, and one plate had warm tea. It was prepared as if Ms. Bell knew that the girls were coming!

"Come children, I've been baking all afternoon. It's not very often that I get visitors."

Ms. Bell's house was beautiful! It was full of color and more importantly, it was surrounded by *PEACE*! You could *feel* it in the atmosphere! The girls wished they could bottle it up and take it home with them! The twins gladly placed their bags to the side and hopped on the chairs. After they crossed the water, Ollie climbed back in the bag and fell asleep.

"Thank you, Ms. Bell!" the girls replied.

Zoey began to munch on the various brownies Ms. Bell had made. Zoey took a glimpse out of the window then looked around the room. She noticed how little there was for entertainment. "You're here in the country; what do you do all day?"

Skylar nudged her sister. She thought that her sister's question was quite intrusive.

Ms. Bell chuckled. "Why, I spend time with *God*! When it's quiet and there aren't any distractions, you're able to hear from *Him* much easier. I truly believe *He's* talking to us quite often; we just aren't listening! For example, if I had a television or was on social media a lot, how much time would I really spend with *Him*? How well could I hear *Him*?"

Ms. Bell smiled. For a moment, she began to think of some of the quieter, peaceful moments she had shared with the *Lord*! The time shared is always so positive and joyful, she began to chuckle.

"Do you get lonely?"

"Zoey!" Skylar shrieked.

"Not at all, my *Heavenly Father* is great company!" Her body seemed light as a feather from the joy she felt in her heart!

"What does *He* talk to you about?" Zoey pressed as she slouched back into the seat and the remaining crumbles of the brownie managed to make its way down her shirt.

Skylar frowned. Her efforts to silence her sister were in vain. She rolled her eyes, realizing that her sister had no intention of stopping her line of questioning. Skylar too lounged back in the seat with her arms behind her head. She knew her sister wasn't intentionally being rude, yet that's exactly how it came across!

But Skylar had to admit that she was curious about the answers to the questions as well. Still, she felt the need to interject. "I apologize for my sister; she normally is not this *nosey.*" Skylar emphasized the nosey part.

Ms. Bell giggled. "No apologies necessary. One can learn much when one asks questions. You would do well to remember that!" Ms. Bell turned her focus back to the question at hand. "*He* tells me when *He's* proud of me and that *He* loves me. *He* answers many questions that I just don't have the answers to. *He* also reveals when I'm right and also when I'm wrong."

Ms. Bell held up one finger to silence Zoey. She knew that Zoey was about to interrupt her. She continued. "And what I need to do to correct my wrongs."

That last part mystified the girls. Ms. Bell still managed to smile, even with the part about her being corrected!

Skylar interrupted with a sour expression. "*He* tells you when you're wrong?"

"Yes, my dear Skylar. The *Bible* says that He corrects those He *LOVES!* AMEN! When He tells me I'm wrong, I know it's out of love, because He wants me to live my life the right way, and to inherit the promise of eternal life!"

Ms. Bell had a glow about her that they had never seen before, not even on Grandma V. The girls nodded their heads in agreement, realizing that this made complete sense! Just as their parents had corrected them out of love, so, does the *Father* correct *His* children!

Ms. Bell continued. "And at times, *He* allows me to operate in the *Gifts of the Spirit* or gives me a prophetic dream! Like last night! The dream revealed that you all would be coming and that you needed my help!" She clasped her hands together in excitement.

"*He* showed you?" Skylar arched one eyebrow in disbelief.

Again, a smile came across Ms. Bell's face as if she was just presented with a banana split with chocolate syrup on top!

Now Skylar was asking *all* the questions and Zoey was certainly noticing! She sat there staring at her sister with her eyes widened.

Skylar lowered her gaze, now a little embarrassed of herself.

The girls were intrigued by what Ms. Bell was saying. They wished they had a close relationship with *God* like she did! *God* revealed to Ms. Bell what their *thoughts* were. She smiled and gently began to braid Zoey's ponytail (which had become tangled with leaves from the woods).

"You can have a close relationship with *Him* too—both of you," while turning Zoey's head towards her. "Seek Him through His word, (*The Bible*) and you will find *Him!*"

She was immediately reminded of why the girls were there. As if someone tapped her, she jolted her body to the side and had a serious expression. "Now girls, I understand you need my help!"

"Oh…yes, Ms. Bell!" Skylar was quickly reminded of the seriousness behind the purpose of the visit. She leaped out of her seat. "We do need your help! We wanted to know if you knew of a cat that could fly and talk?"

Ms. Bell's eyes widened, her smile diminished, and she turned and gazed at her chair sitting in the corner. For a moment, there was silence in the room as she made her way to the chair. She sat down and continued to frown. Her voice now sounded firm, and the intensity of her tone concerned the girls. "There is only one cat that can meet both of those qualifications...her name is *Aurora!*"

Suddenly all the forgotten memories of Aurora came flooding back to Ms. Bell, her frown turned into anger.

"What is Aurora up to now?!" she demanded.

Zoey and Skylar began to speak at the same time. "She came to our house last night and threatened us; she also let off a bad smell!"

"You're lucky that the foul odor is all she did. You girls are powerful, but you don't realize how powerful you are...YET!" she replied in a stern tone with her finger pointed in the direction of the girls. "Until you come to the knowledge of who you are in *Christ*, it will be more difficult for you to overcome your enemies. If Aurora threatened you, she was not working of her own free will. She has a master that has sent her! Whoever her master is…he or she is the real threat!"

Ms. Bell regretted that she didn't have more information. She knew Aurora wouldn't be easy to defeat. Truth was, she was very concerned about the girls!

"We don't know who she belongs to," Skylar explained. "She came alone!"

Ms. Bell had a confused look on her face. "Why have you come to me with this and not your grandma? She too is very wise."

"We know, but we weren't able to reach Grandma Victdamol, and we needed to find out before the cat—I mean, Aurora returned!" Zoey took the liberty of eating another brownie.

Ms. Bell smiled. "You truly are Hartfords. Your family has always been determined, yet impatient. Your impatience quite often places you in situations to work alone instead of together. You're stronger when you work together. Always remember that!"

*And five of you shall chase a hundred, and an
hundreds of you shall put ten thousand to flight;
and your enemies shall fall before you by the
sword.*

(Leviticus 26:8)

In spite of it taking a while, Alexia found another way to reach Ms. Bell's house. Rhonda reluctantly tagged along.

Alexia and Rhonda climbed up on a large tree that overlapped the lake. That tree provided many days of shade for Ms. Bell and many evenings of cool breezes. The tree's branches were long enough that it gently rested on the roof of the house.

Alexia and Rhonda were able to climb the tree and jump on top of Ms. Bell's house! They overheard the end of the conversation.

Who is this Grandma Victdamol that they're speaking of? Alexia wondered. The way they talked about her, Alexia knew that their grandma must be important! The girls quickly got out of sight.

"Lucinda McClaire will know the answer," Alexia informed as if she had been sharing the depths of her thoughts with Rhonda.

- 181 -

Rhonda nodded, despite having no idea what Alexia was referring to! But that was nothing new for Rhonda; she was often left out of the loop when it came to her family! She learned to nod and agree with whatever they said. Disagreeing with them was never an option! She figured if she agreed, she'd be able to figure out later what Alexia was referring to.

"Of course, I'm sure Lucinda Mc-Claire will know," Rhonda agreed.

****

Ms. Bell had enjoyed the girls' company, and she was delighted to see the *faith* that the twins displayed! Prior to Skylar and Zoey leaving, Ms. Bell prayed over them for protection and *wisdom*. She also anointed the girls with oil! They weren't sure what she was doing when she laid hands on them, but all they knew was that they felt peace when she was done praying! Similar to the peace they felt in her house. As the girls were leaving, they waved goodbye to Ms. Bell and headed home.

****

Tammy and Chloe had gotten confused heading back and figured that their sisters would eventually find them. They had leaned up against a tree and unknowingly fell asleep. Skylar and Zoey saw them fast asleep.

Skylar focused her eyes on Zoey, and Zoey nodded her head. "Told you they're strange," she whispered as she approached Chloe and Tammy.

This was more proof for Zoey that something was very wrong with the new neighbors. I mean, what was the likelihood that they would be out there in the middle of the woods—at the exact same moment as her and her sister, Skylar? Zoey was convinced they were up to something—she just wasn't sure what!

She took her foot and nudged Chloe, but she didn't budge! She continued to nudge her harder and harder, but she wouldn't wake up. Zoey leaned in closer to Chloe (with great satisfaction across her face) and screamed in her ears. "WAKE UP!"

Out of all the sisters, Chloe was her least favorite! She complained, always looked angry, and most of all, she insulted the old school video games! So, needless to say, Zoey enjoyed yelling in her ears!

Chloe and Tammy both jumped to their feet. Chloe's immediate reaction was to shove whatever or *whomever* she perceived to be the threat. With one shove, Zoey went flying into a nearby tree.

Skylar stood there for about two seconds in shock at Chloe's reaction! She snapped out of it and ran to her sister's aid!

"Are you okay sis?" Skylar's expression towards Chloe was anything but pleasant.

Chloe brushed the dust off her clothes.

It was now Chloe that stood with satisfaction across her face. She was pleased to see that her *assailant* was Zoey. She didn't care for either twin, but Zoey annoyed her the most!

Tammy knew what her sister was thinking. She knew that her sister's reaction could jeopardize the mission and most of all bring the wrath of Lucinda McClaire down on them!

Chloe saw her sister's horrified expression. Tammy shook her head at her sister, knowing that Alexia wasn't present to wheel Chloe back in!

Fine! I'll play nice! Chloe decided in her head, as she extended her hand as a peace offering. "Sorry. I didn't mean to hurt you. You just frightened me." She lied.

Skylar and Chloe struggled to bring Zoey to her feet, who by the way made no effort to help them!

Zoey wasn't in the mood for apologies. She had a scrape on her knee and now her back was hurting. "Never mind that, what are you doing out here in the woods?" Zoey probed as she surveyed the bruises.

Chloe had no good explanation for Zoey. What was she going to say? *My sisters and I followed y'all into the woods.* She hastily dismissed the thought. She blinked a few times and proposed her explanation as if her purpose there was obvious.

"What does it look like? We were just taking a nap!" Chloe replied smugly as she raised her hands to stretch.

Tammy could tell that Zoey and Skylar for that matter weren't really buying the story. She knew she had to intervene. Operation: *little girl advantage* was in full effect! Tammy plastered on her little girl innocent smile, batted her eyelashes, and pranced around!

Skylar and Zoey were noticeably distracted by Tammy's sudden movement!

"See, I love butterflies, so Chloe brought me out here to find some beautiful colored butterflies. And eventually, we got tired."

Tammy continued prancing around and separating bushes as if she knew the secret hiding spots of butterflies!

"Oh," Skylar observed in a curious tone. How could she argue with such an adorable face? Skylar grabbed Tammy's hand. "How exciting! Did you have any luck?" Skylar managed to match the excitement in Tammy's voice.

"NOPE! Not yet, but I am hopeful," Tammy squealed as she began to skip around a nearby tree.

Tammy was always good—if you will, at making up lies! That was often a *talent* that those in darkness displayed.

Zoey squinted her eyes at Chloe. She wasn't convinced that Tammy was entirely telling the truth, but what was she going to do? Accuse a sweet little kid? That was like the neighbors accusing Abby of something!

Furthermore, Zoey didn't believe that Chloe wasn't aware that it was her when she thrusted Zoey into the tree! Zoey knew she had no proof, so she just stood glaring at Chloe. The tension between the two of them was so thick you could cut it with a knife!

Zoey held her peace as long as she could (which was a whopping one minute).

"What a strange place to take a nap. Most people take a nap in their bed!" Zoey leaned forward with her eyes bulging.

Chloe thought it was best to ignore the comment. After all, she didn't have a good explanation! Chloe began to walk away from Zoey.

Zoey wondered to herself *whether or not they saw them talking to Ms. Bell.*

She whispered in Skylar's ear and asked her.

Skylar responded, "I don't think so. Besides, when we saw them, they were nowhere near Ms. Bell's house."

What Skylar said was true, but Zoey still wasn't so sure! Zoey followed Skylar and Chloe out of the woods.

Zoey's focus went back to Chloe and Tammy. She thought it was awfully strange that Chloe would take her little sister deep out in the woods, just to look for butterflies! So many strange things had been going on lately, she knew she couldn't be fixated on this one event!

Alexia and Rhonda had taken a scenic route in order to beat everyone back to town and were standing in the street waiting for Chloe and Tammy.

Of course, that was Alexia's idea.

"Hey girls!" Alexia called with her hands waving in the air.

"All of you are here?" Zoey had a puzzled look on her face.

Alexia glanced at her watch. "You did say we would meet at 3:00 right? We were meeting up to head to your house. But here you guys are! You saved us a trip!" she replied while smiling and looking down at her watch, knowing that she had deceived at least one of the twins.

Skylar nodded her head. "She's right. We were supposed to meet at 3:00 to go to the mall."

Skylar was waiting for Zoey to respond, but instead—Zoey appeared confused! Zoey couldn't help but notice how the situation was becoming increasingly strange by the moment. *Now all of the sisters were present,* she thought.

Skylar noticed the confused look on Zoey's face. She knew it was up to her to respond. She locked arms with Alexia, "It looks like we all got saved a trip!" Skylar smiled at

Alexia. "Yes, you got the time right! It just slipped our minds." Skylar looked around at all the girls. "But here we are! Perfect timing!"

Rhonda, Alexia, Chloe, and Tammy all nodded their heads. Zoey was still a little suspicious, but the excitement of going to the arcade compelled her to disregard her previous concerns!

The girls were only about 1/4 mile away. Zoey stepped away to call Miss CC to let her know that they were headed to the mall. Miss CC recalled what Ollie told her and said it was okay.

It was a warm summer day. Some kids were outside selling lemonade, others were riding their bikes and playing with water guns.

Amid the mystery of Aurora and the warning from Grandma V, they welcomed some level of normalcy! Skylar took a deep breath as the wind blew through her hair; she wanted to enjoy every moment! She welcomed the opportunity to not focus on good or evil, being a Hartford, or thinking about flying cats! She just wanted to be a *kid*, at least for the day.

"Tag!" she yelled as she unlocked arms with Alexia and ran.

"Oh, really now?" Alexia shouted as all the girls scurried in various directions. "I'm going to get you!" Alexia hollered but Zoey and Skylar were way too fast! She was forced to tag one of her sisters. "You're it!"

"No fair! I'm too little, I can't catch anyone!" Tammy whined.

"Here, tag me!" Chloe extended her hand.

"Oh no! Run!" Alexia and Rhonda yelled.

Skylar and Zoey ran like never before.

Chloe's sisters knew that with her long legs, no one would be able to outrun her!

Rhonda's laughter filled the street. She didn't have many moments of just being a kid. Her family was always plotting and planning. This was a refreshing contrast to what she was used to. She admired how the twins were able to enjoy being kids! They could laugh and have fun, without being ridiculed! She smiled, knowing that she needed to embrace this moment, because she didn't know when or if it would happen again!

CHAPTER 19

IS IT ALL FUN AND GAMES?

The girls arrived at the mall and took a moment to catch their breaths. Zoey had to admit; she was having a lot of fun with the neighbors. Although she wished Stephanie was there, but she had to cancel. She leaned over with both hands on her knees. Everyone was out of breath and embraced a moment or two of stillness.

As they entered the mall and made their way to the second floor where the arcade was, Zoey and Skylar noticed that the arcade wasn't as crowded as it normally would be!

"Are you sure this is the *hangout spot?*" Chloe probed annoyingly with her nose flared. There were just a handful of kids there.

Zoey was embarrassed. "Well, yeah. It usually is. I don't know, maybe it's because the weather is nice, and everyone decided to play outside!"

Skylar always managed to try and look on the bright side of things. "Well, I look at this as a positive! I can *never* play Pac-Man! It's always crowded and not one person is over there!" Skylar took this opportunity to run over to the game in case any of the girls were getting any ideas!

The girls all followed her lead and began to choose the various arcade games.

Chloe and Zoey ran towards Donkey Kong. They both paused for a moment in hopes that the other would relinquish their rights to the machine. After a five-minute standoff, Chloe took a deep breath and reached to slide her game card into the machine.

"Not so fast!" Zoey opposed as she blocked Chloe's game card. Zoey stated the obvious. "Who said you could go first?!"

Chloe began to crack her knuckles; her eyes burned with anger. "Looks to me like I'm already about to play!"

Alexia observed the familiar wrinkle on the right side of Chloe's lip. She knew that it only made an appearance when she was about to *hit* something! From the looks of it, Zoey was about to be her latest target! She brushed past the other girls and ran towards Chloe. Alexia forcefully stood in front of her sister. Chloe was much taller than Alexia— she didn't do much to block Chloe's evil stares as she scowled at Zoey!

"What's going on here?" Alexia asked impatiently.

They both began to *spill the beans* on everything that had occurred. They talked over one another, and Alexia could only make out a portion of what was said. She held her hands up to gesture for both girls to stop speaking. They both obeyed like obedient puppies! "Okay, it sounds like you both want to play Donkey Kong!"

Chloe and Zoey *only* nodded as if th eir vocal cords no longer worked.

"Okay, each of you swipe your game cards and take turns," Alexia stated the obvious! "You can compete against each other. Compare your scores!"

Chloe was not happy! But with a quick jerk to the right of Alexia's head, Chloe realized that once again she was compromising the mission! She didn't want to have to deal with the consequences of disobeying Lucinda McClaire! With her shoulders now slouched, she adhered to her sister's suggestion.

Zoey didn't like it either—but she knew it was a reasonable solution! She was waiting for Chloe's response.

Chloe's teeth gritted, "Sure Alexia, that's a great idea. Why didn't I think of that?" There was obvious sarcasm in her tone.

Zoey and Chloe's anger towards one another quickly diminished. Instead, they engaged in some healthy competition—for Donkey Kong, that is!

Meanwhile, Rhonda was playing Pac-Man with Skylar. She had to admit that Skylar was a lot better than her. After all, she had more practice! Skylar had won the first game, but out of nowhere Rhonda began to surpass Skylar's levels.

"I can't believe I'm getting a higher score than you," Rhonda confessed.

"Yeah, you're pretty good," Skylar smiled as she blew a bubble with her bubble gum.

Rhonda peered over her shoulder and suddenly it dawned on her. She realized that Skylar was *letting* her win!

But why? she wondered. She looked in her direction and Skylar flashed her a gentle smile.

Because that's just the type of person she is, Rhonda realized. *Pretending* to be friends with them wasn't going to be *THAT* hard. Rhonda wasn't used to people being kind to her! Not even her own family. She tossed a quick smile back in Skylar's direction (she hoped that none of her sisters witnessed her genuine display of kindness) and she continued to play.

****

Miss CC was watching Abby play with Shye in the backyard when the twins came in. Zoey tossed the bag down and headed upstairs with Skylar.

"Hi Miss CC!" they yelled as they ran upstairs, hoping to avoid any questions.

Oliver was a little dizzy from the toss. He unzipped the backpack and shook his fur. He had to stay hidden the entire time they were with the neighbors, so his fur had gotten a bit matted. Miss CC knew this was the perfect time to speak with Ollie. She might not get another opportunity for a while. She sat at the table by the sliding glass doors so that she could keep a close eye on Abby.

Miss CC waited anxiously in anticipation of the report on the events of the day! Her smile swiftly diminished when she saw Ollie shaking his fur and looking extremely irritated! She didn't have to wait long for an explanation for Oliver's expression.

"They got some new friends, and they forgot about me!" Ollie stomped on the floor, "What am I, chop liver?" Oliver grunted as he kicked the backpack.

Oliver was reacting in a similar way that Zoey did concerning Stephanie and the neighbors!

Miss CC was used to Ollie being extremely sensitive. She had learned a long time ago that the best thing to do when he was upset was to simply change the subject!

"Well Oliver, tell me what you know," she insisted. "I was here… so I missed everything!" she frowned. But then she perked up, "but you were there for the excitement!" she again insisted. "Tell me everything!"

Ollie huffed and paced back and forth as his colors bounced from black to green to yellow and to orange and so on, (his fur always changed when he became nervous).

"Well, a big cat visited them last night and threatened the family! This cat could talk, and fly and its eyes burned with anger! That's why they had to visit Ms. Bell," he explained as he straightened out his whiskers.

"A flying cat! You should have mentioned that this morning!" Miss CC scolded.

Ollie knew she wouldn't be pleased about that. Miss CC saw sadness on Oliver's face and decided not to fuss any further at him. She placed both elbows on the table.

Oliver's expression was now one of frustration. "And then they met up with those girls from the pool and spent the day with them!"

Miss CC regretted asking. Ollie went on and on about the twins' day and how they paid him absolutely *NO* attention.

****

"That was pretty fun, wasn't it?" Zoey asked.

"Yes, it was. Rhonda was pretty good at Pac-Man!" Skylar admitted.

"Can you believe they never heard of those games?" Zoey continued as if her sister hadn't said a word.

Zoey was always eager to talk about anything pertaining to games!

"No, I can't," Skylar mumbled. She hated when Zoey would ask her a question and then ignored her answer. She had a habit of doing that whenever she got excited.

"Chloe wasn't bad at Centipede. I watched her play from across the room. Who would have thought she'd like a game that shot at things?" Skylar sarcastically replied.

Zoey nodded her head in agreement as she tossed her basketball up in the air as she laid on her back. "She was pretty good at Donkey Kong too," she reluctantly admitted.

"I did hear you had some stiff competition with that." Skylar's eyes narrowed. "Did you win?"

Zoey jolted off her back and sat up, "Of course I won! Do you need to ask? She's good *but* remember—I'm the best!"

The girls laughed. Skylar had a gleam of pride in her eyes for her sister.

CHAPTER 20

LUCINDA MCCLAIRE STRIKES AGAIN!

Alexia, Tammy, Chloe, and Rhonda had returned home as well.

"I can't believe you guys fell asleep! And aside from that, they *found* you!" Alexia kicked her bedroom door open as her sisters followed.

Tammy ignored Alexia's comment. "So, you mean they actually walked on water?" Tammy's eyes were wide with excitement.

Rhonda nodded her head, knowing that Alexia was in complete denial.

Alexia was quiet, she hoped that her silence would discourage her sisters from having any further conversation about the matter.

Rhonda however, considered Alexia's silence as the green light for her to speak up and share her thoughts! Which Rhonda was happy to do!

"Yeah, it was pretty cool!" Rhonda squealed while giving Tammy a high-five.

"Nothing they do is *pretty COOL!*" Lucinda McClaire was standing in the doorway unnoticed. She mimicked Rhonda's voice and shot a cold look in Rhonda and Tammy's direction. Lucinda McClaire's focus quickly turned back to all four girls. Her blue eyes were now full of fury and displayed the color orange.

Rhonda immediately regretted displaying her excitement!

Lucinda McClaire could see the fear on her girls' faces. She liked instilling fear in anyone she could, and her children were no exception! A sinister smile crept across her pale face. Her presence alone managed to shift an already dark atmosphere and make it a tad bit darker.

"I told you girls to pretend to make friends with them, not to get caught sleeping when you're supposed to be spying!" She faced Chloe and yelled.

She pointed her long skinny fingers in the direction of Rhonda. "And don't fabricate stories about them walking on water!" Lucinda McClaire's voice bellowed throughout the house.

Deep down inside Rhonda wanted to protest. She wanted to scream to the top of her lungs that the story wasn't embellished in any way! She wanted to ask Lucinda why they never saw her walk on water! So many things ran through Rhonda's mind, but she dared not speak any of them!

Lucinda McClaire continued. "Do you *actually* want to be friends with them?" She asked as her eyebrows curled up on their own. She directed her question towards Rhonda!

Rhonda's voice trembled with fear, "What, friends...? No, I would never *actually* be friends with them, Lucinda McClaire!" Her eyes nervously dodged back and forth from her sisters to Lucinda, with her eyes ultimately resting on Lucinda McClaire. She hoped Lucinda McClaire believed her. After all, she had never mastered lying, like her sisters.

"They're weak! Worse than that, they're...good! How can I be friends with something I despise? We hate *all* Anointeds!" Rhonda shouted as her voice grew louder with each syllable! Rhonda held her breath in hopes that she convinced all of them. But most of all...Lucinda McClaire!

Lucinda McClaire gazed at her with a smug look on her face and with her eyebrows in a raised position. She looked at Rhonda and Tammy and lowered her chin that had previously held a slight lift. She examined them both for a moment.

"Very well then." She cautiously lowered her eyebrows and tossed her hair over her shoulders. "And what did you learn at the game room?"

The neighbors all turned to one another bewildered, wondering how she knew where they went.

"Oh, don't look so surprised! I know *EVERYTHING* you girls do!" Lucinda McClaire replied with a creepy smile.

She swooped in closer and sat on the ottoman, poised and eager to hear the report. She crossed her legs and stared at them with a slight glimmer of anticipation. "Also, what is this about a woman by the lake?" Lucinda McClaire added.

Alexia was waiting for an opportunity to speak. She circled the room with her hands folded behind her back. "They call her Ms. Bell. She seems harmless enough."

She placed a finger on her chin, as a memory popped in her head like a flicker of light.

"But their grandma, that's who they kept talking about. She wasn't there but she's probably not important." She continued rambling. "And as far as the game room, well everyone did a good job and began to build a good rapport with them!"

Alexia shot a quick glance at Chloe. Chloe knew that Alexia wouldn't tell Lucinda McClaire about the conflict between her and Zoey. Alexia and Chloe were aware that if Lucinda McClaire had previous knowledge of the incident, she would have addressed it the moment she entered the room!

Lucinda McClaire stood up and paced back and forth. She hadn't heard a word Alexia said about the game room. She stopped listening to Alexia once she mentioned *their grandma*. "Their grandmother's name is Victdamol Hartford. As a child, I learned about *THE VICTDAMOL* Legend has it, she is one of—if not THE most powerful Anointed out there. Victdamol Hartford operates in many gifts, no one really knows how many. Some believe that her granddaughters will operate in even more gifts and at a level that even *she* hasn't experienced!"

Lucinda McClaire's plan wasn't to focus on *THE VICTDAMOL*. But this gave her an idea. She knew how to get to the twins. They were virtually untouchable in Oldsville Terrace, but if she could get them away from the city, her odds would be better.

Victdamol would soon be the past of the Hartford family. But Lucinda McClaire was aware that Skylar and Zoey were their family's future!

She clapped her hands together and the sound thundered throughout the room! Needless to say, it got her daughters' attention! She began to walk in a circle in the middle of the room while clasping her fingers together and allowing them to intertwine. "I have a plan to use Victdamol as bait and destroy this family once and for all!" She gazed out the window.

The neighbors didn't dare disturb Lucinda McClaire, when she was deep in thought! They just looked at her, anxiously waiting to hear what her plan was. Everyone except Rhonda, that is!

She then turned around. "I'll just need to bring in a little help." She paused as if someone interrupted her. "Oh yes! A *little help*," she did a creepy laugh. Rhonda didn't know what the 'little help' could mean, but by Lucinda McClaire's excitement, she knew that it couldn't mean anything good for Skylar, Zoey, or their family!

Alexia ran up to Lucinda McClaire, "what do you need us to do?" with enthusiasm in her voice.

Lucinda McClaire patted Alexia on the head. "Keep doing what you've been doing. Get close to them! Gain their trust! When it's time to fill you in...I will."

Just like that, Lucinda McClaire shooed Alexia back to her seat.

Out of all of Lucinda McClaire's daughters, Alexia reminded her the most of *herself.* She was driven and eager to do whatever Lucinda McClaire required. Just as Lucinda McClaire had once been junior apprentice to her mother, so was Alexia to her!

She loved the attention she got from her daughters, but she really liked how Alexia emulated her style and her desire to *do no good.* She opened the bedroom door, and five Javas entered the room! This was the little help she was referring to. One by one, they entered the room with their shools. Alexia, Chloe, and Tammy began laughing. They were familiar with the Javas and how dangerous they could be! On the other hand, Rhonda stood with her teeth clenched, concerned for Skylar and Zoey.

CHAPTER 21

A LATE-NIGHT TRIP!

Skylar and Zoey were determined to find out who Aurora belonged to. They sat at the table in front of their lunch. Neither of them had much of an appetite. They began to make mountains out of their mashed potatoes and raindrops out of their corn.

Miss CC couldn't help but notice their bizarre behavior. "Okay girls, what's wrong?"

They knew they couldn't tell her the truth because Miss CC didn't know who they *really* were. They pondered about what they could say.

Miss CC was aware that Skylar and Zoey were facing challenges. She knew that her assignment was to help them, she just wasn't sure how to! She thought about when she was a kid, and a smile crossed her face.

"Listen girls, when I was a little girl and I needed guidance, my mother gave me a locket. She kept half and I kept the other. My mom told me it would help us find our way back to one another, if we were ever separated. Now you girls can have them both. I'm an adult now and I no longer need it and neither does my mom!"

She placed two gold necklaces on the table. At the end was a locket that was shaped like a compass with a cross in the center of each of them! The girls smiled and took the necklaces. They knew that things were changing quickly and they needed to be prepared from all angles.

The twins could never have imagined how useful the necklace would be for their journey ahead. The necklaces were not just random pieces of jewelry. If the necklace holders get separated, the built-in compass helps them find each other!

It can also guide a person out of the darkest places and direct them towards the light. Miss CC had a history of her own with the necklace. It helped both her and her mother when she was a young child. Miss CC wasn't just *any babysitter*, she had secrets of her own!

****

The girls had received a voicemail on both of their phones from Grandma V. She apparently called that morning apologizing for missing their call and explained how she was outside gardening and didn't hear the phone. Zoey and Skylar realized that Grandma V must have returned the call when they were out in the woods and that their cellphones must not have had any signal.

They tried to return Grandma V's call but there was no answer. They thought it was unusual that Grandma V wouldn't answer at night! They knew she wouldn't be out shopping or doing much of anything at that hour of the night. Although they spoke with Ms. Bell, they still wanted Grandma V's opinion on the matter. Too much had happened, and they knew their mom had no intention of taking them to Grandma V's anytime soon.

The twins decided to go see Grandma V, even though they knew her house was extremely far. On foot, it would take them all night—since they were unable to take the bus because it didn't run that late. Zoey and Skylar were nervous about traveling at night, especially Skylar! But they knew that *God* would be with them!

In addition to wanting to get Grandma V's opinion, they also were a little concerned that they couldn't reach her. They had a sinking feeling that something was wrong! They went upstairs and tied a few bed sheets together and lowered themselves out of the window.

Zoey slid down the rope made of sheets. She went down so quickly that she landed on Skylar's head and they both fell on the ground. Oliver rolled out of Zoey's backpack.

"Oh, I hate dirt," he whined as he brushed the red flowers off his fur.

"Sorry Ollie, I didn't realize I was going so fast."

"I'll say!" Skylar uttered as she rubbed her head.

The girls slowly crept between the rosebushes and potted plants. They made their way to the sidewalk and headed south. They knew that it would take them all night to get there, but they hoped that Grandma V could *pray* the girls right back into bed! Grandma V had always taught them that there were no limitations where *God* was concerned!

The streets appeared much creepier at night. They could hear dogs barking, owls hooting, and wolves howling in the distance. Skylar and Zoey held each other tight as they continued to walk down Lecture Street. Rainn was closely trailing behind.

"Hey girls, why are you out so late? Don't go so fast! Can you just wait?" he called as he ran up to the girls.

"Hi Rainn!" They yelled with large smiles on their faces.

Normally, Skylar and Zoey would be furious that Rainn was there, but they were relieved that they weren't alone any longer. The girls thought about Aurora and what had happened. One thing repeated over and over in their minds.

They couldn't shake what Ms. Bell said, *"You find the owner, you find the real enemy!"*

Skylar and Zoey liked Rainn, but the fact still remained that he was an Undutched, so they couldn't *fully* trust him!

Zoey had a peculiar look on her face. She placed her pointer finger on her chin.

"Hey Rainn... Do you have any pets?"

Skylar shot Zoey a quick look of disgust. She knew what her sister was insinuating.

"Pets? No," he responded while rubbing his ring on his shirt.

"Have you ever had any pets?" Zoey pried.

"Well..." Rainn began to think really hard. "I guess so, if you can count my goldfish, Silver. I got him on my thirteenth birthday."

Zoey shook her head. *No, it can't be Rainn. No offense, but he's not that clever,* she thought to herself.

"Where are you girls headed this time of night?" Rainn asked.

"We've got to check on our grandma." Skylar replied.

"Are you gonna walk the whole way to Coconut Grove?" He began fishing through the green and yellow bookbag he was carrying.

"Why do you walk when you can fly? Why don't you cruise through the sky!" Rainn pulled out a small bench with balloons for wheels!

They giggled at how funny the contraption was. The bench was brown with four huge red balloons under it. It began to change to the normal size of a bench. The bench hopped from side to side.

"You better hop on before you miss your ride!" he warned.

Skylar and Zoey were aware that Grandma V didn't like Rainn very much. But they also knew that it would take all night to reach her house. Zoey tucked Oliver's head down in the book bag. "Don't be scared Ollie!" she whispered.

Ollie rolled his eyes for two reasons; he hated being put in a bag and he still didn't like Rainn.

The girls leaped on the bench, and it continued to hop from side to side. It picked up speed and ran down the street. Skylar held on to Zoey, Zoey held on to Rainn, and Rainn held on to the bench as they all leaned back as the force of the wind blew against their faces. The bench was headed straight for a house.

"We're going to go right through their door!" Skylar cautioned.

Everyone braced themselves for the hit, including Rainn! Right as the bench approached the door... up, up, up they went! Each of them slowly opened their eyes. The bench had several balloons that helped it fly!

They yelled as they flew over the house. The sky was dark with the exception of the moon and stars providing a ray of light. Skylar and Zoey enjoyed the view as well as the breeze that forcefully pushed their bangs out of their faces.

"You know, each one of those stars have names," Rainn exclaimed while pointing to them. It was as if a star heard, and it shimmered.

"Wow!" the girls were in awe.

They crossed over the *Welcome to Oldsville Terrace* sign. They could see Miss Margaret's Famous Pizzeria and the local bowling alley! Everything was so beautiful from the sky; even the local dump site's stinky truth was hidden amongst the night.

CHAPTER 22

GRANDMA V, WHERE ARE YOU?

Peepop had awakened and leaped off *their parents' bed.* She headed down the hall, but not before satisfying an itch on the tip of her nose with her paw. She meowed at Skylar and Zoey's room, but no one came to the door. Peepop strolled down the stairs and jumped on the counter. She gazed out the window and looked towards the sky.

It was as if she knew the girls were somewhere out there! Abby came down the hall with her bunny slippers on. Abby wasn't lifting her feet, so her house shoes made a sliding sound across the floor.

Peepop turned her attention towards the noise. She jumped off the counter and crept on the side of the couch with her back raised and tail spiked as she waited to pounce on whatever was making the noise! She tilted her head down a little to see who the perpetrator could be. The sliding noise came closer and closer and finally Peepop saw pink bunny slippers.

"Meow!" she screeched.

Abby was so frightened that she dropped her favorite teddy bear—Buttons, on the floor.

"Huh!" she yelled as she stumbled over one of Nick's toys. Abby fell on her bottom. She saw Peepop's head peeking from beside the couch. She laughed as she made her way over to Peepop.

"Silly cat!" she whispered. "You scared me! Let's go get you some milk!"

Peepop followed Abby back into the kitchen.

Aurora was watching them through the window and Shye ran into the kitchen and started barking at Aurora!

"You're going to wake Mom and Dad up!" Abby warned.

But Shye just kept barking!

"That mangy dog is going to ruin everything!" Aurora screeched as she flew away.

"What is it boy?" Abby asked as she peered out the window, but Aurora had already left! All Abby could see were the streetlights shining dimly on her driveway. She reached down and picked up Shye.

"There's no one out there boy! Why don't you sleep in my bed tonight?"

* * * * * * * * * *

As the girls came closer to Coconut Grove, the bench came to a halt at the end of the dirt road. Their grandma's house sat off in the distance. There was a faint lantern in the window that glowed as if it was leading the way in the dark! Rainn assisted the girls with getting off the bench.

"Thanks Rainn," the twins said in unison.

"When you girls are in need, have no fear. Out of nowhere, I'll be there!" He waved goodbye and jumped back on the bench and flew away.

They all knew that Grandma V would not be pleased that Rainn was there, so it was best for him to leave!

"I don't think Rainn is all that bad." Skylar's gaze moved to the ground. "Grandma V might be wrong about him," She hesitantly suggested.

Zoey nodded her head in agreement.

As the girls drew closer to Grandma V's door, they stepped onto the porch, and it made a creaking sound.

"Grandma's house is a lot scarier at night," Skylar noted.

The girls raised their fists to knock on the door, but the door instantly flew open with just a gentle tap!

They entered the house and Grandma's parrot squawked. "She's not here! She's not here!"

Zoey quickly looked around the room. "What do you mean she's not here?" Zoey asked. "Grandma V is here! Where else could she be?" She inquired as if Penelope could answer her questions!

The girls walked around the house, but they couldn't find Grandma V anywhere, in spite of it being the middle of the night!

The door was unlocked, only a small lantern was lit, and Penelope was left all alone! This made no sense to Skylar and Zoey!

They knew Grandma V would not leave without telling them.

"Skylar, look! I found a note!"

The note read:

HELLO EVERYONE! I, GRANDMA VICTDAMOL, MUST GO AWAY ON A VERY IMPORTANT MISSION· I DON'T KNOW WHEN I WILL BE BACK, BUT THE MISSION IS TOP SECRET· I WILL CONTACT YOU WHEN I RETURN·

-GRANDMA VICTDAMOL

Zoey placed the note in her pocket.

"Well, I guess something came up! I'm sure she'll be back soon."

In spite of what the note said, Skylar *discerned* that something didn't *feel* right! It was unusual for Grandma V to leave in the middle of the night to go *anywhere*! She never went out at night, if she could help it! Not to mention her note sounded almost *robotic.* It didn't sound the way Grandma V would normally address her family!

She spun around and looked at her sister with concern on her face. "Grandma V wouldn't leave and not tell us! Especially when she believes that we could be in danger!"

"Skylar, maybe that's just it! Maybe she went to go find out about *the danger,* you know—to protect us!" Zoey suggested.

"Grandma V always says to follow your instincts, and MINE are telling me something's wrong!!" Skylar's eyes darted in Penelope's direction. "Besides, we both know she would never leave Penelope here all alone! There's no one here to take care of her!"

Skylar scanned the room for any clues. Penelope was in her cage, swinging back and forth looking at the girls with one eye opened and the other closed.

"Now that's true," Zoey admitted. She stuck her finger in the cage and assisted Penelope with pushing her swing back and forth.

Skylar continued to look around. She moved the newspaper that was sitting on Grandma V's favorite chair, but there was nothing there! There was, however, coffee in the coffee mug sitting on the table. Beside the coffee mug were two other cups with hot chocolate in them. Grandma V lived alone so there would be no reason for there to be three cups!

She picked up the coffee mug, which had coffee inside that was barely touched!

"Way to go Skylar, a coffee mug is a great clue!" Zoey joked.

Skylar resented the fact that her sister was so dismissive of her concerns. She ignored Zoey's remark. She held the mug in her hands. It was still warm and so were the other two cups!

Skylar perked up. "Grandma V hasn't been gone long; her cup is still warm!" Skylar was in the zone! "Do you think someone came to visit Grandma V?"

Skylar continued as if she was the only person in the room. She proceeded to ask questions, not really expecting her sister's input.

She had a confused look upon her face, "but I will say, if someone came that she didn't want to," while inspecting around the room once more, "she certainly wouldn't offer them hot chocolate."

Skylar poured one of the cups of hot chocolate down the drain. Worry clouded her face once more, "But who would visit Grandma V in the middle of the night?!" Skylar grinned, "Aside from us of course!"

Zoey's face grew with concern with each passing moment. She now realized that her sister may be right! Zoey was feeling a little ashamed. She should have shared the initial concern with her sister, instead of joking around!

"I don't know, it's not like she has any neighbors close by," Zoey finally spoke up as she gazed out the window.

"Maybe, just maybe, it's not Grandma V who fixed the hot chocolate," Skylar supposed as she began to bite her nails.

"Stop it, Skylar! You won't have any nails left at this rate!" Zoey pulled her sister's fingers out of her mouth.

Skylar forced her hands in her pockets. It was a nasty habit that caused her much embarrassment. She had tried to stop, but to no avail!

"Look at this!" Skylar walked past her twin. She noticed their grandma's walking stick over in the corner.

"Now we know the letter isn't from Grandma V!" Skylar threw her arms up in the air. "Now tell me, where could she go without her walking stick?" Skylar held the stick in her hand and stared at her sister while waiting for a response.

Zoey began to realize that the possibility that Skylar was right was increasing by the second!

Zoey's eyes swelled with tears. "Do you think something bad happened to Grandma V?" She waited in anticipation of her sister dismissing her concerns.

Skylar rushed to her sister's aid, "it's going to be okay," now realizing that she was scaring Zoey! "Grandma V is very strong!"

The girls went into Grandma's room, and everything seemed normal. Nothing was out of place. Her robe was hanging up, and her favorite book—*The Bible*, was beside her bed! The bed, however, was not made up; it appeared as if it was slept in.

"This room doesn't look like Grandma V was about to leave! Her bed was slept in, and all of her clothes are in her closet," Skylar observed as she moved the clothes around.

"Maybe someone disturbed her sleep," Zoey suggested.

Skylar saw a dim light shining under Grandma V's bed. She lifted the corner of the bed spread and grabbed the item.

Skylar picked it up and showed it to Zoey.

"It's a shool! It looks just like the one we saw in the practice world!"

"The Javas must have been here!" Zoey shouted.

"One thing's for sure; they didn't want to hurt her—otherwise, we would have found her injured or..." Skylar paused for a moment and continued. "That could only mean one thing...they have her!"

Zoey's eyes lowered.

Skylar lifted her sister's chin. "But that's a good thing! That means they need her!"

Zoey nodded her head and wiped her tears away! She knew what her sister said made perfect sense! Aside from her theory lining up, Zoey always viewed Skylar as the 'smarter' twin.

Skylar's eyes lit up! She ran towards the cups. Zoey *knew* that look meant one of two things: either Skylar was putting the pieces of the puzzle together or her sister was about to be the winner of Monopoly! And there certainly weren't any board games around!

Zoey followed her sister. "Skylar, what is it?!"

Skylar paced back and forth across the wooden floorboards. "They must have used the shool while Grandma was asleep, and the Javas were probably waiting on someone and made themselves some coffee and hot chocolate while they waited!" Skylar faced her sister. "The only reason Grandma V had hot chocolate in the pantry was for us. We all know she's a coffee drinker! She absolutely hates hot chocolate. There must have been a minimum of three Javas here, since there's three cups. By the temperature of the cups, they couldn't have been gone for more than thirty minutes or so!"

Zoey was impressed by how her sister was able to put so many pieces of the puzzle together!

Once again Oliver had fallen asleep, right after reaching Grandma V's house. He woke up yawning and stretching.

"What did I miss?" he asked with heavy eyelids.

"Ollie, the Javas took Grandma V. They must have gotten her when she was sleeping!" Zoey looked panicked again.

"What!" Ollie yelled. Ollie had heard about Javas before; and no way was he eager to make their acquaintance!

Skylar stuck the shool in her pocket.

"There's got to be some other clues around here." Zoey crawled on the ground searching to see if any other clue was left behind.

The girls surveyed the house. Nothing else appeared out of place. They made their way back towards Grandma's room and on the nightstand the letters *NE* were written on a piece of paper. It was definitely Grandma V's handwriting, but it seemed as if she was about to write another letter and was interrupted.

"NE? What was she trying to tell us?" Skylar placed her pointer finger on her chin.

"I don't know but we've got to find out!" Zoey said with determination in her voice.

"Girls, we've got to go...! They could be coming back!" Ollie warned while glimpsing around nervously.

Skylar and Zoey realized that he was right! They grabbed Grandma V's parrot and ran out the front door. They made their way across the dirt road, over the gravel, and to the street!

Zoey was gasping, "Now what?" She was initially met with silence from Skylar and Ollie. "I guess we have to start walk-ing!" Zoey groaned.

"Well at least we only have to walk one way." Skylar had a healthy habit of looking for a silver lining in everything!

Rainn appeared from behind an oak tree. "I thought you girls may have needed me to stay, so I only pretended to go away!"

The girls ran up to Rainn and hugged him! They were grateful for his help! As they hopped on the bench, the shool fell out of Skylar's pocket, but none of them noticed!! They held on tight and headed back to Oldsville Terrace.

CHAPTER 23

THE PROOF IS IN THE PUDDING!

The girls pulled the sheets that they used to climb out the window—back in. Rainn was sitting on the bench outside of their window.

"Rainn, you always manage to show up when we need you!" the girls recounted with a grateful smile.

"Don't question why. If you need help, just know...I'm your guy!" Rainn smiled and waved goodbye.

What the girls didn't know was that the rock Rainn gave them not only symbolized following *Jesus,* it was also a tracking device! In addition, if at any time the girls were in any distress, it would detect it! Through the rock, Rainn could locate the girls, in case they needed his help!

"I suppose, we can't do this alone!" Ollie reluctantly admitted, "I wasn't the biggest fan of Rainn, but he *has* been there to help you girls!"

"Yes, he has!" Zoey agreed.

Skylar was still focused on the events of the night. She put her nightgown on. "We can't tell Mom because she won't believe us, and if she doesn't believe us, Dad definitely won't either!"

Skylar and Zoey wanted to be able to depend on their parents. But unfortunately, as their mom grew further away from *God*, she became less reliable when it came to spiritual things! This meant that when things came up, they knew that they would be faced with a barrage of doubts and questions. Questions they didn't have the answer to!

They could barely believe that their mom was the one who taught them about *God*! It wasn't so much about what their mom *said*, it was how she *lived*. She used to live a surrendered life to *God*! She included him in everything! But one day something changed, and so did their mom!

Zoey shook her head with disappointment in her eyes. "I know Skylar; it looks like it's up to us!"

"Zoey, this is way too big for us. We've got to get help from someone!"

"Why don't you tell Miss CC? She can help a lot more than you think. And you can definitely trust her!" Oliver sat on the edge of Zoey's bed kicking his feet. He knew that Miss CC could help the girls. Now if only he could convince them to confide in her!

Zoey and Skylar's eyes were filled with doubt.

"Just trust me!" he pleaded as he gripped the covers with his paws.

They knew that they had to be careful about who knew their grandma was missing. She was the most gifted Anointed left, so all the Hazils could view this as an opportunity to attack. The girls weren't sure who they could trust. They agreed to speak with their parents in hopes that they might share their concerns.

****

Skylar and Zoey woke up extra early to catch their parents before they left for work. Skylar was watching television in the family room. The constant changing of the channels began to annoy an already nervous Zoey!

"Skylar, I know you're anxious, but can you find one channel and leave it please!" Zoey pleaded as she walked back and forth, towards the window.

Skylar peered over her sister's shoulder. "It looks like I'm not the only one who's nervous. Just what exactly are you searching for outside?" Skylar attempted to follow her sister's gaze.

The weatherman had not predicted any rain, but the wind was howling, and the clouds were moving in fast!

"It's gonna be a bad one," Zoey observed.

The girls never liked storms, especially when their parents wouldn't be at home to comfort them!

"Good morning!" Their dad walked in the kitchen and poured some orange juice, and their mom was right behind him. She was yawning and stretching.

"Why are y'all up so early?" she asked.

Oliver was hiding behind the stairs. He didn't believe it was a good idea for the girls to tell their parents. He preferred that they speak with Miss CC, but they had clearly made up their minds.

Each twin grabbed their parents' hand and led them to the kitchen table. Their mom and dad sat down with puzzled looks on their faces.

"Well, you're out of school so it can't be about a bad grade," Dad joked as he drank his orange juice.

"Skylar and Zoey, if this is about your babysitter, you girls aren't old enough to stay home alone," Mom protested.

"Oh no! Miss CC is great!" the girls clarified.

Zoey cleared her throat and was laser focused on her parents. She swallowed deeply. Butterflies danced back and forth in her belly. "Mom, Dad, Grandma V is missing!"

Skylar nudged her sister. She couldn't believe that Zoey blurted it out like that!

Both of their parents paused and stared at one another confused. The girls waited on the edge of their seats for their parents' response!

Would Mom burst into tears? Would their dad have to comfort her? Or would Dad run out the door like a superhero looking for answers? they wondered.

Their parents turned to one another and burst into laughter.

"Girls, my mom missing is like misplacing an entire house! Mother doesn't just go missing, she's too wise and you girls *know* it!" Their mom stood up and poured herself a glass of orange juice and gently tossed a couple of ice cubes in the glass.

Skylar and Zoey grew frustrated at their parents' nonchalant attitude.

Skylar reasoned in her mind that desperate times called for desperate measures! "We visited her last night, and her coffee was still warm. Her parrot was left alone, and it just didn't seem right!" Skylar blurted out with tears rolling down her face.

As soon as the words came across her lips, she knew it was a BIG mistake! Skylar and Zoey could visualize steam coming out of their mom's ears!

Their mom stood up with anger in her eyes.

"WHAT DO YOU MEAN YOU GIRLS WENT TO MOTHER'S HOUSE LAST NIGHT!!" she hollered.

Zoey nudged Skylar on the shoulder.

Their dad quickly realized that for Skylar to share that information, it could only mean one thing, they were really concerned about Grandma V! Their dad walked over to their mom and held her hand, and it immediately calmed her down.

"Sweetheart, we can find out how and why they visited her later. Right now, why don't you call your mom and check on her?" He gazed at her with comforting eyes.

Their dad was always the voice of reason. He had a knack for calming their mom down when she was just about to go off the deep end.

She reached in her purse for her cellphone while staring at the girls with anger in her eyes. She shook her head in disappointment. Mom did an occasional gasp and grunt as she waited for Mother to pick up.

Grandma V's voicemail came on. She still had a landline with a voicemail that could be heard throughout her house.

"Now, now Mother... Stop teasing the girls and show them that you're okay," she requested, but there was no response.

"MOTHER, tell the girls that you are okay!" she yelled.

Their mom's face began to grow with concern. But that lasted for just a moment. She dismissed her previous concerns, hung up the phone and grabbed her briefcase. "I don't have time for Mother's games! I have a job to get to!"

Zoey reached in her coat pocket and handed her mom the note left by Grandma V.

"Why didn't you show me this sooner? It says RIGHT HERE that she will be gone for a while." Mom responded as she pointed to the words on the paper.

"Mom, when has Grandma V ever gone anywhere without letting us know? Besides that, she didn't take any clothes and her bed was unmade!" Skylar pleaded.

It was as if a light bulb went off in Skylar's head. She suddenly remembered about the shool.

"Oh, and we even found one of the Javas' instruments!" Skylar reached in her pocket with excitement in her eyes, knowing that this was the proof they needed!

Their mom had learned about the Javas as a young girl, and this intrigued her! *Now* the girls had her attention! She considered the possibility that they just *may* be telling the truth! She stood there waiting anxiously for Skylar to show her the shool.

Skylar felt around in her pocket but for some reason they felt empty. She glanced at her parents and her sister who appeared very impatient. *It has to be here,* she thought. But it was nowhere to be found!

Skylar turned to her mom, whose face was growing redder by the second.

"Where is it, Skylar?" Zoey nervously tapped her feet while occasionally glancing at her parents.

They both knew this was the proof they needed to get their mom on board.

Skylar's voice began to tremble "I...I...I don't know where it went!"

Skylar's tone elevated to a shout, and she turned to her sister. "I put it right here!" She pulled out her pockets, revealing they were empty! She then turned to her mom. "It was right here! I promise!" she said with tear filled eyes.

Their mom shook her head from side to side. She was disappointed in herself for almost *falling* for one of Grandma V's *tricks* (or so she thought).

"Did Mother put the two of you up to this?" She was certain that her mother convinced the girls to be a part of some *plan!*

Skylar and Zoey turned to their mom with deep concern in their eyes as they shook their heads *no*.

Very well. Perhaps they aren't in on it, their mom thought to herself. "This is nonsense, Mother is fine!" she barked as she walked out the door with Nick following closely behind.

Both girls turned to their dad for comfort. He didn't know what to believe!

"It is her mother, and she knows her better than we do. Maybe she is just out of town," he turned back to his daughters, "or perhaps she *is* playing a joke." He kissed the girls on the cheek and waved goodbye as Miss CC ran inside to get out of the rain.

"That's one heck of a storm, isn't it?" Dad remarked as he took Miss CC's rain jacket and hung it up.

"It certainly is! The news didn't say anything about rain, much less a storm!" She took her yellow umbrella and leaned it up against the wall near the door.

Miss CC couldn't help but notice Skylar and Zoey's long faces.

Skylar pulled Zoey into the living room as their dad was speaking with Miss CC.

"Maybe we *should* tell her," Skylar whispered.

"No, we shouldn't!" Zoey replied firmly.

Oliver came hopping over to them, "Now what?"

Miss CC closed the door and ran into the living room where the girls were. She could tell that the twins were worried about something. She wondered if it was the same *something* she was concerned about! Miss CC knew that *now* was the time to *talk* to them—to tell them the truth!

"Girls I have to share something with you! I'm not just a *babysitter*. I am a close and dear friend of Miss Victdamol."

Skylar and Zoey both turned around with their faces lit up!

Miss CC continued. "You girls realize that she wouldn't trust just *anyone* to watch over her jewels!" she revealed with a gentle smile.

Oliver was relieved that Miss CC finally revealed the truth to the girls.

They smiled. They were relieved that they no longer had to deal with this alone!

Miss CC motioned for both Skylar and Zoey to go in the kitchen, and she made her way to the refrigerator. She pulled out peanut butter and jelly and got a couple slices of potato bread. They sat on the stool and Oliver stood on the edge of the counter.

"I am sharing this with you because, I haven't been able to reach her! When she never returned my calls, I decided to visit her. I think something is wrong," she hesitantly informed the girls.

Miss CC didn't want to alarm them, but she needed to find out what was going on and she thought they may be able to help!

Skylar and Zoey leaped into Miss CC's arms!

"Finally, someone else who's concerned about Grandma V!" Relief came across Skylar and Zoey's faces. "We were at her house too and we know something has happened to her!" they explained.

"So, who exactly are you—really?!" Zoey asked.

Miss CC pushed the sandwiches to the side and leaned in closer, so she could be eye to eye with Zoey and Skylar.

"My family are Anointeds as well!" Miss CC glanced around as if someone or something could hear what she was about to say, "But, we don't have the same calling as your family does. We don't fight in physical battles, though we do assist those that do!

We've recognized that your family specific-
ally was chosen by *God* to go into battle—
when called. Helping all of you is an assignment for us. Even Oliver is here to help the
two of you!"

Zoey peeked over at the yellow umbrella in the corner. She was finally comfortable enough to ask a question that had
been nagging her ever since they met Miss
CC. "I know it's raining today, but even
when it doesn't rain you have this umbrella,
why?"

Miss CC walked over to the umbrella. "I was given this umbrella for protection. If I am ever under attack, there are
very few things that can get through the
umbrella. It's basically a large shield!"

"Why would you be under attack?"
Zoey asked.

"Unfortunately, anyone who is an
Anointed or on the side of *good* is considered
a threat."

CHAPTER 24

STEPHANIE'S MISFORTUNE!

*If the world hate you, ye know that it hated me
before it hated you. If ye were of the world, the
world would love his own: but because ye are not
of the world, but I have chosen you out of the
world, therefore the world hateth you.*
(John 15:18-19)

There was a knock at the door. Skylar, Zoey, and Oliver were startled by the
knock. *Who could that be?* they all wondered. But no one said a word!
Miss CC slid the sandwiches over to the girls
and gave them a reassuring smile.
    "Stay put, I'll be right back."
    Stephanie was standing at the door
with a large lollipop in her hand. The

lollipop was so large that it nearly covered her entire face.

Miss CC opened the door.

"Hey, you must be the babysitter, I'm Stephanie." She quickly introduced herself and blew past Miss CC to search for her best friends.

Stephanie wasn't very comfortable talking to people she didn't know. Now with her friends, she could *talk* all day long!

Miss CC watched the young girl stick her head in various rooms, she was searching for her friends.

She could have just asked me where they are, she thought. Miss CC yelled, "the girls are in the kitchen!"

Stephanie threw her hand up in the air and headed to the kitchen. Miss CC was so fixated on Stephanie that she didn't realize that two Javas *snuck* in the house behind her.

"Hey Steph! This really isn't a good time," Zoey was stuffing her mouth with the peanut butter and strawberry jelly sandwich.

"Yeah, we're a little busy," Skylar agreed while enjoying her peanut butter and apple jelly sandwich. "How could she know which jelly flavor is our favorite? Wow she's the best!" Skylar remarked.

Stephanie shook her head from side to side. She placed her arms around their shoulders. She had to admit, the thought of her friends being a little jealous did manage to put a smile on her face.

"Still mad at me, huh? Listen, there's enough of me to go around. I can be friends with the new neighbors as well. After all, you girls are my *best* friends! Besides, I have a peace offering." she reached in her bag and handed them a chocolate bar each. This was also her way of apologizing for canceling on their outing to the arcade.

"I was never jealous." Skylar clarified as she placed her hand on her chest and looked in her sister's direction.

Zoey had no intention on admitting that she didn't want to share her best friend! She quickly dismissed the conversation.

"Great Steph, you're our best friend too, but it's still not a good time," Zoey insisted as she took the candy bar out of Skylar's hand and shoved them both back in Stephanie's.

"Hey, I wanted that," Skylar squealed.

Stephanie was confused; she couldn't understand why the girls didn't want to accept her gift. Zoey knew that if they took the candy bars, Stephanie would never leave! She would have to tell the story of how she came across her large lollipop! And how she managed to stop to the store and find their favorite chocolate bars!

Zoey led Stephanie back to the foyer.

"Sorry Steph, but this just isn't a good time."

Zoey knew they had a lot to discuss with Miss CC and they needed to concentrate on finding Grandma V!

Stephanie wondered if the girls were still upset with her despite her gleaming smile and peace offering!

Miss CC had picked her umbrella up to shake the rain off that got on it earlier. She grabbed a towel out of the hall closet to wipe up the water.

As Zoey led Stephanie to the foyer, she was patting her on the back. Suddenly, two Javas appeared. One was pointing his weapon at them!

"Oh no! Javas!" Zoey yelled as she forcefully knocked Stephanie to the ground.

Abby had just woken up. She heard voices downstairs and was headed to join in on the *fun*! She strolled down the stairs, rubbing her eyes. Her timing couldn't have been worse!

The female Java was not too far from the stairs! She saw Abby and ran towards her with the shool and pressed a button! The red light Grandma V warned them of, shot out! The light was headed in Abby's direction, but Miss CC opened her umbrella just in time to shield Abby from the red light!

Skylar and Ollie heard the screams and made their way to the foyer.

Since when do I run towards danger? Oliver wondered.

Miss CC grabbed Abby and locked her in a closet. "Stay here," she whispered.

The female Java chased Skylar around the couch.

"Don't be afraid! You're an Anointed!" Ollie shrieked as he ducked under the coffee table.

Skylar and Zoey suddenly recalled the training Grandma V did with them!

"What's going on?!" Stephanie screamed as she dropped the lollipop and began to crawl on the floor. "And how is *that* rabbit talking?!" she squealed with her eyes widened.

Zoey began to pray for *God* to intervene! Just then, Skylar and Zoey could hear a soft voice.

The voice exclaimed, "Resist the fear and *fight*!"

The girls tossed pillows off the couch and towards the Javas. One by one, they were cutting through the pillows with their shools.

"Stay down!" Skylar warned Stephanie.

But Stephanie was too afraid! She had only wished that she had listened to Zoey earlier and left when she first suggested! When she saw an opportunity, she made a run for the backdoor! One of the Javas saw and pointed the shool in Stephanie's direction! The red light came out and she fell to the ground—stiff!

"No!" Zoey yelled. She became enraged first, but suddenly she felt empowered! Her heart was overwhelmed with *faith*, and she held up her hands and stated, "I command you both to leave in *Jesus'* name!" She spoke the words with faith and authority!

Both Javas immediately disappeared!

Skylar turned with her eyes widened and anger upon her face! "What did you do?!" Skylar yelled. "Now we'll never know where they're keeping Grandma V!" She elbowed Zoey. Zoey was surprised at Skylar's reaction! They had never put their hands on each other before. Zoey knew that for Skylar to react that way she must have been really scared for Grandma V!

Zoey embraced her sister and whispered. "I'm sorry. You're right, we could have interrogated them."

Skylar stood there for a moment; stone faced—but she didn't remain that way for long.

Skylar was immediately convicted for yelling and elbowing her sister. She knew Zoey didn't mean to interfere with them getting Grandma V back. Zoey was only trying to protect them! She immediately turned around and hugged her. "No, I'm sorry for hurting you and yelling at you." Skylar responded with a gentle smile.

"Don't worry, you didn't elbow me hard at all. It's more so my feelings that were hurt," Zoey explained.

The twins embraced one another. Zoey glanced over Skylar's shoulder. She could see Stephanie lying on the floor.

Zoey motioned towards Stephanie. They both ran to their friend's side. When the girls touched her, it appeared as if she was frozen.

"Oh my gosh! Miss CC, we've got to get her to a doctor!" Skylar cried.

Miss CC was looking at the ground with the weight of her body swaying from side to side, "A doctor can't help her." Her eyes shifted back and forth between the floor and Stephanie. "This is *spiritual,* not *natural*," Miss CC exclaimed.

"What happened?" Zoey squinted her eyes.

"That weapon has a light that freezes a person. That's the same light they tried to use on Abby." Miss CC explained.

The girls had forgotten all about their little sister. "Abby!" they called.

She came running out of the closet and hugged her big sisters with tear-filled eyes.

Their attention turned back to Stephanie, now knowing that Abby was okay. The girls didn't know what to do about Stephanie. They knew that the Java used the shool in the same manner that Grandma V warned them about!

"Maybe now Mom and Dad will believe us!" Skylar was crying.

Zoey plopped down on the sofa and buried her face in the pillow. She was frustrated with her parents for not believing them, afraid that they wouldn't find Grandma V, and upset with Miss CC for not telling them sooner who she was! She didn't know what to do. To make matters worse, she hated to admit it, but Skylar was right. By banishing the Javas, there was no way to know who had Grandma V and where they were keeping her! She felt as if she had let everyone down!

Skylar knew how Zoey was feeling. She put her arms gently around her twin's shoulder. "Everything is going to be okay."

They did not have many options. The girls knew that after seeing Stephanie, their parents would believe them now! This made them happy, though at the same time it caused them some concern.

Whoever took Grandma V, whatever this *danger* was that Grandma V was warning them about, now seemed more REAL than ever! Grandma V was now missing, Stephanie was frozen, and Abby almost ended up the same way! The girls began to ponder whether or not telling their parents was a good idea! They could after all be putting them in danger by doing so. Were they willing to risk something happening to their parents too?

"We can't tell Mom and Dad!" the twins blurted simultaneously.

"Wait, I'm confused girls. Your mom's an Anointed and your dad's a Miran... They can help!" Miss CC expressed while picking Abby up.

"Yes, we know...maybe they can help." Zoey was confusing herself.

Skylar interjected. "We can't risk their safety." She faced her twin. "We've got to do this on our own. Besides, Mom and Dad haven't had a relationship with *God* in such a long time. Truthfully, I'm not sure how much they could really help anyway!"

Miss CC stared at Stephanie and then focused back on the girls. "I understand."

It was left up to them to take everything Grandma V taught them and put it to the test!

****

Their parents were leaving on vacation, and Miss CC was going to be in charge of the girls for the next five days or so. They felt that this may have been the best thing, after all, Miss CC understood what was going on and she *believed* in them! And most of all she knew that *God* would be with them!

Miss CC placed her arms around them.

"We will find your grandma and get your friend healed; all will be well again," she assured as they laid Stephanie in the guest room.

Miss CC had great confidence in the girls, and she was aware that Grandma V had been training them! She also knew about the power of the weapons of warfare, and she believed the girls would be equipped to deal with their enemies.

It took them the rest of the day to clean the room and put everything back in order. Just as they were placing the fallen lamp back on the desk, their mom and dad came through the door.

"Hello girls!" their mom shouted.

Perfect timing, they thought.

Skylar placed her finger in front of her lips and motioned for Abby to be quiet!

She didn't want Abby to slip up again! Their dad walked in and hugged them.

"Girls, we're going to pack. Oh, and we're taking Nick with us as well. You sure you girls are okay with not coming on this vacation? Mom and I would love for you three to come," Dad said.

Zoey and Skylar's idea of fun wasn't exactly traveling from state to state, visiting gardens and museums.

"No—we're good! No offense but we'd rather stay! But thanks again for thinking of us," Skylar said. Besides, they had more important things to focus on!

Their parents headed upstairs to get ready!

They were relieved that their little brother was going to be gone, too. He was one less person they would have to worry about!

"Miss CC, we don't even know where to start," Skylar whispered.

They had little clues to go on.

Miss CC took the girls into the kitchen and pointed towards the sliding glass doors which faced their backyard! Skylar and Zoey had a puzzled look on their faces.

"You want us to go in the backyard? How is that going to help us?" Zoey's fore-head was wrinkled.

Miss CC continued to point—but she pointed past the yard—beyond the woods and over the swamp, deep into the forest, and towards the peak of a mountain!

The girls swallowed deep and lou-dly; they had always been told to stay away from there! That place was known as Ricketts Valley! Grandma V always told the girls that there was nothing good in Ricketts Valley! Part of them wanted to believe Miss CC, but on the other hand they believed that maybe—just maybe, it could be a *trap!*

Miss CC continued. "That is prob-ably where they are keeping her. I know you girls were probably told to stay away from that area." Miss CC's eyes softened. "The reason is because people say that the Javas, Hazils and all of the Anointeds' enemies meet beyond that swamp! If they have her anywhere, it's probably up there!" She poin-ted back towards the mountain with a grimacing tone.

The girls could never see beyond the woods as a result of the thick trees. But *there* was the peak of a mountain high in the sky. They had always heard weird, roaring sounds coming from that mountain! There was often banging, voices, and squeals coming from up there as well! At its peak there remained a dark cloud hovering over it, even when the sun was shining elsewhere! It was as if the mountain never permitted the sun to shine on it!

Abby had been listening to everything from the hallway. She ran up to Zoey and Skylar. "I don't want you guys to go!" Abby cried. "It's too dangerous!"

Zoey looked at Abby as tears ran down her cheeks and she embraced her. "Forget about it! We can't go up there!" Zoey walked out into the backyard.

"We have to Zoey! That's probably where Grandma V is!" Skylar pleaded as she followed her sister outside.

"We don't even know what's up there!" Zoey pointed in the direction of the mountain.

Zoey always feared that mountain! She had always thought about all the different scenarios of what could be up there, and now *they* were telling her she had to go *to* the mountain!

"We have no choice, Zoey and Abby! We have to save Grandma V. Besides, *God* has not given us the *spirit of fear.*"

Suddenly, a *supernatural* peace came over Zoey and Abby!

"Don't worry, you won't be alone; I'll be with you too!" Ollie remarked as his tiny paws reached for Zoey's hand.

Mom and Dad came down the stairs all packed, with Nick in toe.

"Girls!" Mom called.

Oliver placed his back against the wall to stay out of sight. Abby, Zoey, Skylar, and Miss CC entered back into the house. The girls hugged their parents and Nick and said their goodbyes.

"See you in a few days!" Mom and Dad shouted as they left.

Miss CC went into the kitchen to make the girls more sandwiches and pack drinks for them to take along with them on their journey.

"What do you think, Skylar? Can she be trusted?" Zoey asked.

"What choice do we have? She's the *only* other person who believes Grandma V is in danger!"

Miss CC entered the room in the midst of their conversation. "Well girls, there isn't much time! Your parents will be gone for many days, but the journey is still long."

Miss CC hurried the girls to the door. She pushed their hair behind their ears and stood for a moment staring at them as if they were her own little ones! Tears filled her eyes, but she fought them back. She cleared her throat. "Okay girls. Use the necklaces I gave you, and you will never stay separated from each other for long!"

Skylar and Zoey looked at one another and then at Miss CC.

"You're not coming?" they asked.

Miss CC stroked Abby's long pony-tail. "Sorry girls, I can't. I have to stay with Abby. Besides, my calling is not for physical battle."

Skylar and Zoey had completely forgot about Abby. And they certainly weren't willing to put their little sister in any danger by her tagging along!

Miss CC knew that the girls had a mission that they needed to complete together. Fear crossed Skylar and Zoey's faces. They didn't want to admit it, but they were afraid! Miss CC *sensed* their fear and placed her arms around them. Truth was, she was a little nervous for them as well! However, she knew she couldn't make her feelings known!

"Your grandma has taught you girls enough to defeat your enemies. All you need to do is have *faith* in *God*! *He* will never leave you nor forsake you!"

Miss CC grabbed the olive oil out of her purse that had been prayed over. She placed a dab on their foreheads! She prayed for the *God* of Abraham, Isaac, and Jacob to watch over them, protect them, and to guide them. This gave the girls great comfort; they could recall when their mother used to anoint them with the bottle of oil when they were younger!

"Don't forget. I'm going too!" Ollie confirmed as he stood on his tippy toes for Miss CC to pray over him as well!

Zoey picked Oliver up and held him close. "Thanks Ollie," she whispered.

Miss CC smiled in agreement. This made the girls feel a little bit better. She got the oil and prayed over Oliver as well!

Miss CC stuffed food and juice boxes in their bags. "This should hold you!"

The girls weren't happy about traveling so close to evening, but they knew that the journey would take days, and they needed to figure all of this out before their parents returned.

Aurora pressed her ear against the glass and had been listening to them the entire time. She overheard that they were headed to Ricketts Valley. Aurora was familiar with the area. She had an owner many years ago that lived on that mountain!

Even Aurora was afraid to travel back there, but she knew that she had to listen to whatever her master told her. Lucinda McClaire wanted her to follow the girls and report back to her. She knew that she had to unfortunately make a trip to Ricketts Valley!

As the girls waved goodbye to Miss CC and Abby, they walked down the concrete driveway in the direction of the peak of the mountain!

Zoey began looking all around her from one side to the next.

Skylar wondered what her sister could be looking for; she began searching around her as well! "What are we looking for?"

"I was just hoping that Rainn would pop out of nowhere and come along with us!" Zoey nervously chuckled.

Skylar and Ollie nodded their heads in agreement.

Zoey wrapped her arms around her sister, and they began their long journey to find Grandma V!

THANK YOU!

First and foremost, I give all praises and glory to my Heavenly Father, Jesus Christ, and the Holy Spirit! Thank you for guiding me along the way with this book.

To my family, who have always encouraged me to follow my dreams, your support is invaluable! I can't forget my editors and cover art designer; you all are amazing!

A big thank you to everyone who has purchased my book! Words can't express how grateful I am! I hope you enjoyed my novel, and I look forward to coming out with book two of *The Anointeds!*

Also, if you enjoyed *The Anointeds,* please take the time to give me a rating on Good Reads and Amazon! It is much appreciated! Thanks again for your support.

ABOUT THE AUTHOR

This is T.H Land's debut novel. She developed a passion for writing at the age of 8. Her 5th grade teacher, Mrs. Allen entered her into a writing contest! At this event, she had the opportunity to meet several authors, let's just say it was the spark that started her journey! She has always remembered the encouraging words of Mrs. Allen, who first acknowledged her gift for writing! She's grateful for the opportunity to pursue her love of writing while glorifying God through it!